Trigger Warnings

This lil' co-bomination contains scenes of violence, gore, sex, biphobia, rampant ageism, & oodles of creepy-crawlies. There's way too much poop talk for one of the author's taste; but do you, booboo.

Otherwise, it's pretty fucking wholesome. If any of the above offends you, (especially the wholesome part) mayhaps look elsewhere. We hear *Verity* is a real winner.

XOXO,

Phrique + Asher

IN THE CLURB WE'RE ALL MONSTERS

A TRASHY SUPERNATURALS SIDE QUEST

PHRIQUE   ASHER DARK

Dedicated to

our would-be detractors:

Enjoy the show.

Chapters

Fuck Around, Find out

Phrique

Where u @?

Why your generation chooses to abbreviate the written word when it is entirely unnecessary is beyond me.

Fuck yo written word. Where the fuck are you? Don't play with me.

I am at the Coldstone Creamery, picking up the apple of my eye's favorite ice cream so he doesn't act like a sniveling child all night.

Awww. Right answer. Cherry Cake Double Take, EXTRA cake. How sweet of you to bring me dairy. Might as well swing by Walgreens and grab me some Lactaid too unless you want me to be pootin' all night.

Loving you shows my innermost masochist. You are both a joy and a pain to me in so many ways, my little ambivalent time bomb.

Yeah yeah yeah fancy word man, hurry up. You makin' me miss my stories.

Isn't there something you should be working on?

Damn him, he's right. I just wish my executive dysfunctioning wasn't functioning on all cylinders. I switch between my same four apps for a few more compulsion loops, then place my phone on the charger. *Locked Screen* with my *FOCUS* app on. In the name of self-care and the unrealistic illusion of protecting my ever-elusive peace.

I could feel the claws of overstimulation shredding my overworked brain. I was getting distracted, once again by all the pretty colors on my toxic yet addictive phone–knowing I had a list of 9999 things to do. What should I do first? I could start that one story? Which story? One of the 9 anthologies I agreed to? My first collab, maybe, but with whom should I bestow the honor? I worked on Dorian's commissioned art work last night until my eyes barely focused on my Ipad screen. I don't even want to look at it right now.

I should go work out. My back hurts, though. *Carrying around all this talent...*oh wait, no. Save that for your next post. Write that shit down before you forget—wait. Forget what? How long have I been staring off into the abyss?

I hear a slam behind me, making me jerk my shoulders in anticipation of *the killer.* A sharp pain instantly shoots up my neck, an ice pick in my brain. I attempt to calm my panicked mind when my caucasian ancestors whisper for me to investigate what that noise was. My condo is usually brighter than the surface of the sun, but for some reason, I chose today–the day of my imminent death–to try using the desk lamp only. I peer behind me and creep closer to the open door; my brown ancestors are screaming to reconsider these actions. Flicking on the overhead ceiling fan light, and immediately, my heart begins to pound in my ears. My eyes widen and scan the office. I should have known. I asked the universe a question and it sent me back a resounding answer. It was strewn around the walls. My biggest fear multiplied. The horror stared back at me. I look down at my feet to discover what caused the noise. My face contorts into an ugly look of shock and abhorrence.

"The Mime!" I scream as the pain invades me.

"I totally fucked up my neck." I wince as I lean down to pick up my copy of "The Mime" by Tony Profumo. Apparently, the universe's answer was making it so I could barely turn my head and give me the time to finally sit down and read one of my thousand-plus books.

"Boy bye," my attention makes me say as I dust off the vintage horror paperback and place it back where it belongs, examining the walls of shelves full of only one of my many true obsessions. All of their spines staring back at me spitefully, knowing I might be caressing them *someday*.

You mythomaniac! You do nothing but lie, deceive, and eat hot chips!

They all scream at me in a chorus of disembodied voices.

"Some day," I whisper, turning off the light.

I can go draw something. Stop wasting my god-given talent? Tease the cat? Ponder existence? Go check on Wendy Williams? Find a recipe for tres leches cake?

I haven't ridden my $1000 OneWheel skateboard in a while; now's as good a time as any. Right?

Cuz my pussy pops severely! repeats and echoes through my spacious condo. I try to pretend I didn't hear it, I try to push the captivating siren song that is my phone notification out of my head.

But that's a text noise! That's special! We need to see what it is! Distraction! DOPAMINE. GIVE IT TO ME NOWWWW!

I cross the room, downcast and crestfallen, knowing that my overly critical mind is right. I am powerless to my worst addiction. *Of many.*

"Alright!" I yell out, surprising even myself. I see the notification on my screen as I step closer. I see a barrage of text bubbles from names my brain deems typical and unremarkable, but one stands out to me the most.

Hey bitch! Long time no see!

Wanna go smoke?

A vexed look crosses my very minimally creased (from stress, NOT time) face. *The audacity of this ho. knowing I haven't heard from her in over a month. As if I am ever allowed to be forgotten or (gasp), taken for granted?*

My head is a swirl of zippy comebacks and shady back-handed compliments. I need to reply to her immediately, in the name of comedic timing and maintaining *the brand*. While I ponder just the right slicing retort, I glance down at my reflection in my screen and see a shadowy figure coming up behind me.

"I messaged for you to come get your ice cre-" was all I heard before my delayed *fight-or-fight* response engaged, and I decked my on-again-off-again boyfriend, Dorian, in his too-good-to-be-true face.

Three FULL Pumps of Mocha Swirl Mother FUCKERS!

Asher

I stare at my dry phone, yet again, left on read. The audacity of this hoe. I know he's probably pissed that I crawled into my hole—where I can be my no pants, no-bra-wearing crybaby self. People are exhausting. Sometimes, I just need a break. I suffered a great deal of trauma with my last friend group, and needed to pull back from everyone. I needed to recharge my battery. Boy, did I pick the wrong fucking time. My month-long hiatus happened to be right before my bestie Phrique's new book release, *Scissor Me Timbers*. The most lesbian book I've ever laid my eyes on. Reminiscing when JJ would hilariously complain about the nun porn that he *had* to watch for "research," and his extra-ness made me a bit sad. Damn, I missed the fucker. We were both old, stubborn hoes, but he refused to believe he was a day over twenty-one.

My hair-flipping bestie who swore he didn't do the "white girl mkay" when he turned his head quickly, making his hair snap like one of those damn fans he got me addicted to.

Our last convo didn't go so well. I hated his fucking boyfriend and he wasn't a fan of mine. Dick be making us hoes crazy sometimes.

A long, thick one that tickles my guts. That's what I like. He has to be able to move though. A big dick is just a whale on the beach if you don't know how to use it. I don't always want to do the work, I just want to lay there and have my guts rearranged.

The sound of my flatulence echoes from the toilet throughout the bathroom and I giggle a little. *Gotdamn that stank.* I definitely needed to shit. I am not a bougie bitch. Unlike my friend, I can talk about things like taking a dump and not be embarrassed. I have 14 aunts- all of them short, round, and loud. Raised in the projects and trailer parks— much like myself—these women are something to behold. They are loud, brash, and have no filters with zero fucks to give. Hell, my Aunt Pat wrestled alligators! We are strong, trashy women that don't care what other people think. Though tough, they were always there when you needed them. My Aunts would never let a person go hungry and refused to let anyone be alone on a holiday.

JJ was the opposite of my loud trashy family. We called ourselves the odd couple because he is super-duper-fuckin-bougie and I am unlike any woman he has come across. His mama raised him to believe women didn't poop or have assholes. She made him prim and proper. Imagine his horror when he had to share a hotel room and bed with me at an author/book event. *The farting, loud mouth munchkin.* I made sure to keep my poots to a minimum when our good Judy, Judith was in the room though.

JJ and I are completely different, but we work. I will ride or die for my bitch, forever. That is, if he could just get over himself and answer the fucking phone. I knew I was going to be the one to reach out first, but I am ok with that. *I need my friend back.*

Scrolling through Tiktok, going down a political wormhole. *I can't stand Orange Palpatine...* *Scroll Scroll Scroll* *Piece of shit I.C.E. raids!* More political shit, more protests. *I wish I could join more,* the No Kings Day protest was amazing. *Scroll Scroll*

Ohh someone singing! I am obsessed over shows like American Idol and The Voice. If someone could sing well I would cry like a fucking baby. Literally sobbing. Yeah, I know sometimes I can be a lot. *Fucking Geminis.*

After five minutes of doomscrolling, I go back to my regular feed of mostly other authors and book reviewers. The Tuxedo Mask theme song, from my favorite anime,

Sailor Moon, blared from my tiny Samsung speaker. I hated fucking iPhones. I couldn't work them and they aggravated me. I will forever be an Android user. *Fuck what y'all cunt nuggets think.*

I smile from ear to ear as I look at the text.

Dorian:

My Dearest Thumbelina, is there anything I can acquire for you as I make my way to you tonight?

Asher:

Ey Bay! Can you pick me up some Newport 100s and a medium iced latte with three pumps of mocha swirl? Make sure you say the three pumps, make sure they are full pumps. You know what color it's supposed to be. If it's too light, then it's not enough. If it's too dark, then they got that bitch too chocolaty.

Them Dunkin' bitches loved to short a hoe. They don't let the pump come all the way back up before they hit that shit again. When I say three pumps of swirl, I want FULL PUMPS. But sometimes there is too much, like bitch, this isn't a fucking chocolate sundae. Shit be so thick it looks like doodoo sludge at the bottom of my gotdamn cup. I worked at Dunkin' for three years so I know what the fuck I'm talking about. Don't fuck with my mocha. I will turn into a Karen quick if you fuck up my latte.

I sit my phone down and wipe my ass a ridiculous amount of times, then use a fresh wet wipe to make sure I got everything. I'm obsessed with being clean and I go through some toilet tissue quicker than my wax, *aka dabs,* and I smoke A LOT of wax.

Satisfied that my brown eye is clean and pink again, I flush then wash my hands at the sink.

> I will make sure that your order is accurate. How about a carton? That should be sufficient for a week's worth. Ah, I will make it two, just to be on the safe side. I do not want my darling to go without her vices.

When he talked all fancy like that it tickled my cooter. I couldn't wait to bury his face in my cunt when he got here tonight. His sex was fucking amazing. One could say it was almost supernatural. I craved it like my damn cigarettes.

His fancy schmancy words are what stuck the hook in my jaw.

I was in the horror section of my favorite bookstore cafe, *Flick the Bean,* sitting in my favorite blue chair, devouring the latest Patricia Briggs novel when I noticed a man exit the Historical Fiction section. Our eyes met for a brief second then I put my nose back in my book and continued reading on about Charles and Anna, my favorite main characters.

I was once again sucked into the intensity that was Charles. *If you've read the books then you know what I'm talking about. If not, just know he's a hot werewolf that's basically the boogyman to other wolves; who are bad.*

I stayed there all day and ended up finishing the book. The next day I return with my laptop, ready to get some writing done. The cafe gives me peace and it helps me get out of the house; *I'm trying to get better at that.* Sometimes I would sit in my bedroom for months, barely coming out. I just didn't like the world. People have shown me that humans are the real monsters. Having JJ aka Phrique *if ya nasty*, in my life has helped a lot. He basically dragged me out of the house and helped me come out of my shell. I'm sure he regrets that now, because I am a lot sometimes. Then again so is he. I blame mine on being a Gemini though.

I can be very sensitive but I hide it well. My anxiety is almost always on ten. I have moments where I go nonverbal, or I say too much and sound incoherent. My friend knows how to reign me in, but not in a way that would make me defensive.

Anyway, back to how I met my man.

I was sitting at my normal spot, writing what I thought would be my next big project, *Lucifur*. My tiny sausage fingers were tapping away, when a man cleared his throat.

I continued typing but looked up and lo and behold, it was the cutie patootie from the day before. Our eyes locked for the second time and I knew I would fuck this man raw. My cooter called to him like a siren song of queefs.

Slut shame me all you want but this is 2025, honey. Bitches be fucking too. Ain't nothing wrong with being good at bouncing that ass on some random guy's cock meat sandwich. How'd you think you got here? Also, the amount of big booty bitches I've fingered is in the hundreds. They called me jackhammer back in the day. You figure it out. I am pansexual which is something I've had to explain to my bestie a million times now. I don't give a fuck what you identify as. That's not a factor when I like someone. It's all about personality. I'm not like bisexuals. I'm attracted to ALL genders.

"Working on a paper?" His British accent rolled through my body. That was the hook, catching me right in my pussy.

"Nah I ain't in school, this is my current book I'm writing. I'm a horror author. This one has a bit of fantasy mixed with extreme horror elements."

That piqued his interest. We had an hour-long conversation about my writing, which then turned into him asking me to write his memoir.

"I feel like the fates have brought us together. It *must* be you who writes it. I have had far too many years on this earth, and there will be many, many more. To not share my experiences and failures would be imprudent of me, yet I lack the technological fitness required in this century. I long for the days of typewriters, but every publisher I've contacted required manuscripts to be emailed."

That was him reeling me in. I was the big-mouth bass, and he was the fisherman who had years of practice in pole mastery.

I laughed at the nickname because it was fucking true. I couldn't type worth shit on these fucking phones. Maybe my fingers move too fast—plus, they are tiny and chunky—just like me.

I realized I'd been standing in the bathroom like a zombie for fifteen minutes, lost in my own head, when I picked up my phone again.. At the same time, a notification playing rave music fills the bathroom. That's what I typed into Zedge because I don't know the name of the shit JJ listens to, but it reminds me of rave music; just faster and crazier. It's probably called something *extra* like *GabberDisco* or something. Every time he puts that shit on, I can't help but bob my head and wish I had glow sticks to wave around. Even more so now, since the bitch finally texted me back.

MOM! DON'T READ MY SEX SCENE!

Phrique

"Is the ice cream ok?" I asked callously.

"My nose! You—fuck! My beautiful nose!" yelled out Dorian as blood trickled down his once-pristine face.

"Well, why you goin around sneaking up on mofos, Dorian?" I say, my anger and fear dissipating, trying to hide my embarrassment whilst making sure nothing gets on my expensive couch.

Dorian's face doesn't look too bad. My bark is much worse than my bite. I lead the lil' crybaby to my bedroom and have him sit on my black sheets while I tend to his wounds. He continues to sniffle and yowl like a pissed-off cat while I pop in the bathroom to grab the first aid kit.

As I reach into my mirrored medicine cabinet, I notice my level of *dishevelry* and am floored. I forget what I initially went in there for and tussle my jet black (ain't no grays. Did I stutter? Your Mama got grays, ho) wavy hair that hangs down over the left side of my shaved head, just over my ear. I do a deodorant check, confident I'm safe. I throw on a spritz of LUSH Calacas spray, because I want to always smell like lime green jelly beans. Just as edible, but only sweet if you deserve it.

"And stop fucking with your hair!" barks Dorian from the other room.

His voice sounded like it was comically coming through a kazoo. I return to him, looking at me sourly, while still holding his nose. He already sounds better. Well, his voice sounds less nasally and irritated, at least. I'm on clean-up and manipulation duty, so I straddle his lap with a smirk and sit my face within an inch of his. He can't help but be charmed by my chutzpah as I dab his minimally bloodied face with peroxide on a gauze pad.

"Oh no! I busted your lip too," I say with a little more sorrow than might have been necessary, as I dab them too.

Dorian's face is stoic, unmoving, watching my every move. His olive complexion, so close to my caramel skin, was the perfect complement to our matching dark brown eyes. His windows to his soul held mystery, mine held the perfect cover for the ever-so-cunning trickster. I could make a man and ruin him twice as fast. He just had to pay attention to the game and play accordingly. Now was my time to amp it up a notch.

"The best part of you, too. I'm sorry, Daddy," I coo. I pull the pink-tinged gauze away from his face and place little kisses on his tender, swollen top lip. The corners of his mouth turn up slightly as he brings his powerful arms around my ass and holds them there for safekeeping. *Hook, line, and sinker.*

"The best part of me?" he asks coyly, pulling me closer to him.

He smells like the inside of a cedar closet and a hint of tobacco, like money. I gently plant a few more kisses on his lip, letting my tongue poke out and leave a little shimmer before I pull back from him.

"Above the waist," I say in a tempting tone, attempting to land this plane.

I shift as my leg begins to slip, feeling the effects of my schemery growing beneath me. I decide to up the ante by challenging him to a duel as our pork swords riposte against each other. His resolve is paper-thin. One more thrust from me would break him, but what fun is that?

I slide back and off of him, rising as we both stare at his rigid trouser tent. His face looks more fiendish than disappointed.

"Let me get some ice for that," I say, as I walk out of my bedroom, knowing his eyes are glued to me as I leave. I grab the bag of softened ice cream off the floor and chuck it in the freezer as I grab an ice pack for our ailing patient. When I return to him, he's already taking his shirt off.

If I were able to assess his facial injuries, I would have noticed his nose was no longer swollen, and his lip had already begun to knit itself back together. Lucky for him, I couldn't take my eyes off his mitties, the valley between them, and the tent I left behind; still intact. He scooted up on my bed, inviting me to return to the job at hand. A wind blew through the room and magically whipped my shirt off, too. It must have been a freak occurrence, a freak of nature; regardless, Dorian and I had evened the score.

I crawled back on top of him, letting the ice pack trail his torso as I straddled him again. He rested on his elbows, unable to keep himself from smiling.

"Is our patient feeling better?" I ask, trying to keep the slutty male nurse role play going.

"A little," he says, "my mouth could use some attention, though."

At this point, I noticed the swelling didn't seem so bad; his split lip from before seemed barely visible. Still, I gingerly placed the ice pack on his lip like the medical professional I was. Dorian winced a little and gave me a wink, sliding his hands down and digging his thumbs into the waistband of my bummy house shorts. My eyes lit up as our patient motioned for me to take them off, bringing a hand to hold the ice pack in place while I did my best to maneuver them off seductively.

That went out the window as I practically toppled off him, tangled in my own hoochie daddy shorts. We both chuckled at the irony of the sexy attire basically thwarting any tantalization points I had accrued thus far as I finally threw them aside. Which left just me, my boxers, Phrique Jr., and the sexy man whose mouth I was aching to impregnate behind.

He nestled closer to me, propping himself up on one arm to face me. He pulled the ice pack away from his mouth and grinned at me.

"How do we look?" he said innocently.

The cut wasn't even visible anymore, just soft, pouty lips that I loved watching when he talked.

"Fuckable as ever," I said, pausing as a pang of guilt hit me in the gut. "Do you forgive me?"

"Just this once. Now I know not to sneak up on you, or at least guard my face if I do."

"I'd never hit ya. It's just sometimes you make me angry, see."

Dorian makes a disgruntled face. My joy deflates a little.

"*Strangers with Candy* reference," I say, certain that a misfired joke just ruined my chance of getting laid again.

"We don't do domestic abuse. What are we, a couple of breeders?"

Dorian chuckled, so I knew I still had a shot.

"Oop. Forgot you're half half-breeder. My bad."

At this, he pursed his lips and looked me in the eye again.

Womp-womp.

"You do remember that I'm opening a bisexual club, right? Your bisexual schtick probably won't be tolerated as well by those who don't find your irreverence as intoxicating as I do."

"For as much as I like boobs and find dudes gross most of the time, I'm probably a bisexual too-"

"So why don't you join us and claim it? It's freeing."

"...I already had t-shirts made that say Queer as Poptarts. Queer, outlandish, eldritch. It just works. Wait, I thought your club was just pro-hedonism? How does that translate to being bisexual?"

"How much easier would it be to reach life's ultimate pleasures than by doubling your odds at finding it?"

"You should make the theme *sandal night,* for a room full of flip-floppers. Ok, sorry, that's my last bisexual joke. I *sweatergawd.*"

"That mouth of yours is going to get you in trouble someday."

"With the bisexuals? Or just you?" I can feel him smirking at me. He loves the show. "Cuz I know how to use it for good too," I say, cranking up my brown eyed, cherubic grin to level 9000.

"Why are our clothes still on again?" I said, as Dorian pulled me into him.

Our lips meet in a tender kiss straight out of a wholesome romcom. Then he slides his tongue in my mouth, and the electricity flows straight to my cock after a quick pit stop at my nips. I'm still wrapped up in his arms with my breath quickening when he rolls us over. We stop with him writhing on top of me, his warm body blanketing me as our temperatures continue to rise. I part my legs, letting him nestle in between as we take turns sucking on each other's tongues. His hands slide down my glistening torso, curving around so he can scoop my ass up. He's dragging his nails along my sides as he frantically pulls my suffocating boxers off me. His cock is bobbing and prodding against my taint and ass, like a hungry bear's snout digging for man honey. I let a guttural grunt of anticipation vibrate next to his ear as I lift my hips up to assist him. He's already pulling as he aggressively swoops down to finish the job. He meets my thrusts with his mouth engulfing my throbbing tent. Precum is already soaking through, but he's sucking at the fabric like it's his last dying meal. A groan rolls out of my gasping mouth as the back of his teeth pulls against my dick head, and he successfully gets my boxers out from under me.

Before I even have the chance to finish pulling my ankles free from my boxers over his head, Dorian is already nuzzling and slurping at my cock. I throw my head back as the waves of pleasure hit me. I run my hands through his thick brown curls, balling my hand into a fist every time I feel his tongue twirling. All I can do is lay back and enjoy, bucking my hips here and there, stunned silent other than the passionate grunts and moans. Someone told this man the secret, *the only way to shut me up,* and he took that as a challenge.

He comes up for air, letting junior slap and glob against my stomach, while he pulls his arms around my legs enough to get a firm grip on them. Our eyes meet, and he gives me that devilish, ravenous wolf stare. My head is a wash as all my viable blood flow is being diverted to my pleasure centers below. I feel his hands pressing against the back of my knees and the air hitting my ass. I'm jolted out of my titillated daze when I feel his lips and tongue lapping at my hole. His tongue eases and probes deeper while his hand snakes around and pulls on my cock at the same time. Junior dribbles precum down his blurring fingers as he continues to pump my shaft. I grab my other leg, and he thanks me by darting his tongue deeper into me. His breath is furiously forced through his nostrils as he buries his tongue deeper into my inviting hole.

At this point, I'm seeing stars. My fun parts are a musical instrument he knows how to play all too well. His fingers and tongue are hitting every button my body needs to bring my throaty moans to a fever pitch. My breath catches in my throat as my body begins to tense. He lets my shaking legs drop, standing over me as he strokes his already stiff, dribbling dick. He pulls himself closer, teasing my ass with his raging cock, letting both our juices comingle. A drop of precum glistens on my tip that he swoops down and catches in his mouth. Slurping up and down, gagging and taking me deeper down his throat than he's ever been able to before, bringing me closer and closer. My body tenses again, but he doesn't stop, my moans get louder, and my thrusts into his mouth become more frantic.

Our eyes meet again, and I see the glimmer from another world. I'm too wrapped up in the throes, delirious from my body taking over as hot spurts of my cum shoot into his waiting mouth. Suctioned to every ridge and curve of my anatomy, slurping up every drop. I shudder as the tremors from my climax roll through me, and he lets my spent cock drop from his skilled mouth.

"Fuuuuuckkk" was all I could utter, feeling like I just had my life force sucked out of me. I jokingly shut my eyes, feigning sleep when-

I woke up seven hours later to a text notification.

That was a regretful cum & go, but I had to work out a few things with Igor before Friday. Dreadfully sorry that I had to put that juicy ass of yours to sleep, but it's the only way I know you'll actually sleep. Be a good boy today.

I rise, throw on a hoodie & grab my boxer briefs off of the ceiling fan blade. *That was all him. I was trying to focus on the sexual healing of it all.* I slip them on after relieving my bladder. I finished getting dressed, glancing over to make sure he didn't leave any money on the nightstand. *Just in case.*

I wouldn't have hated it if he had spent the night. This club opening has been taking up a lot of his time. I just hope he doesn't overwork himself. Always on the go, always working on something, wondering why his lack of sleep and moderation was slowly catching up with him. *That sounded hypocritically familiar.*

I grab something bougie, fruity, and electrolyte-y to drink, having depleted more than a few with my significant *otter. Ooh, post-coital ice cream!* I think, but quickly scold myself.

Not until we accomplish something, get something done, finish something!

Ugh, we're so mean.

Oh no, not talking in third person??

Are we catching feelings for this man?

Or was this just the afterglow talking?

Oh shit, I hope I backed up Dorian's commission before that lascivious manhandling.

I grab my iPad and take a huge sigh of relief. The cloud auto-synced when I plugged it in to charge. I take another look at it, reasoning that a freshly-fucked set of eyes might allow me see things from another perspective. Perhaps a color needed to be tweaked. Maybe his nose looked too big. Maybe I didn't get the arch right on those soup-coolers of his.

I compare the rendition I was currently drawing for him to the few stills I took. It looked just like him, just a bit more *debonair*. I definitely captured that devilish smirk correctly. I stare at it a bit longer before I save it again. I love it. I just don't fully trust my eyes. I need to show someone else who might look at it from a different perspective. I reflexively screenshot it and pull up Asher's name to text it to her, when I realized I never responded to her! *Damn you muscle memory and damn you ADHD. In my head, I had already responded to her hours ago.*

New phone, who dis? Certainly not someone who forgot I was alive for like a year??

I type...but don't hit send yet.

Alright girl, it's not that dramatic. You weren't exactly an angel during y'alls last little exchange.

I scroll up and read our messages from a month ago. For nostalgia, a memory jog, and a little autosadism.

Asher:

> Look, I just don't get along with your man. That's all. We don't gel. He always has to say something slick about my smoking and he always makes a face when I fart.

JJ:

> Jekyll is very particular about smells. Can you blame him? You're the same way! There's only so much Sweet Pea body spray you can hose yourself down with. We can still smell it. This is just because your man is a freak about it. Y'all are WEIRD.

Asher:

> Bitch. First off, it's Japanese Cherry Blossom. Second, Hyde loves everything about me. Even my nervous stomach. Get you a real man like mine, not that nerdy little *gaycel* you hitched your wagon to. Bitch, are we fighting?

Bitch, yes, we are! Jekyll is a nerd genius. Do you know who the next billionaires are? The nerd geniuses! I'm tired of paying my own bills, ho. It's about time I got to be a kept man for once, like the real housewife I was born to be. So go and have fun with your lil' burnout Hyde & don't text me when y'all both need to get bailed out of jail.

[Tiktok link sent minutes later of Asher dancing & clapping her ass angrily to Kelis' *I Hate You So Much Right Now* with no reply]

I shake my head, *Damn, we so dramatic,* and finally reply to her.

Yeah, sure. Why not? I could use a drink anyway. <3

4

Big Dick Daddy wit tha Caaaandy Stick

ASHER

Oh the bitch decided to text me back, finally. A very vague and unlike him message, however. Where was the sass and the smart ass comments?

> You agreeing so easily has me scared to meet you anywhere that isn't a public setting. You might be trying to take me out bitch.

> BIIIITCH! STOP BEING SO PARANOID! I may or may not miss you. Who else is going to deal with all of this?

I know he is gesturing at himself. I need to be high to deal with him right now. I set the phone down and grab my favorite purple and black Seahorse Pro Plus dab rig. It's purple with black speckles on it. Two of my favorite colors. I used to roll blunts, but I've leveled up and become bougie with my Mary Jane. I like wax now. It was cheaper, lasted longer, and was more potent than flower. Blunts taste nasty to me now. Even a fucking bowl tasted like ash and dirt, no matter how gas the shit was or how fruity my plug says it was.

Opening the lid of my wax holder, a circle silicone jar that's about an inch high, I use my metal tool to move it around and pack a bit to the side. It's sticky like you would expect, but mine was more crumble than batter.

Tapping the button on my dabber three times, I wait for it to stop blinking, then hit it a few times. I started coughing and gagging when I accidentally inhaled it too hard. *Jesus fucking cat nipples, too much.* I continue to cough, and my eyes water as I start gagging.

Oh fuck! It's coming back up!

I run to the sink and spit out the vomit that forced its way through my lips.

Jesus, Mary and hoe sis! That shit's got me higher than a giraffe's pussy, I think to myself after I rinse my mouth out and stare at my red eyes in the mirror.

Back in the small living room of my apartment, I plop myself on the couch, phone forgotten, making amends with my friend who may be trying to lure me out to kill me, forgotten. I fell asleep watching last night's episode of Love Island; my man also forgot.

I awake to someone rubbing my booty. Smiling, I turn over and look at my love, Dorian, holding my iced mocha latte.

He was warned only once on how to wake me. The first time I opened my eyes to him in my face I reached out and touched him, and not in a good way either. I smacked the taste out of his damn mouth.

Don't be in my face waking me up!

And don't talk to me as soon as I open my eyes. A bitch needs a minute before all that yapping.

The only thing that will wake me up in a good mood is a booty rub, and my boo just so happened to be the best at it.

He waits for me to talk first, like the good boy he is.

"I got so damn high I done fell the fuck to sleep. My bad, boo."

Grabbing my drink from him, I take a sip. Perfect. They actually made it right this time. The perfect amount of espresso and chocolate.

Damn, this is good. I set it on my nightstand and gaze at his skin that's darker than my pale, red, and blotchy complexion. He looks at me with those intense dark eyes and starts to unbutton his shirt. My eyes follow his every move as he undresses, one article of clothing at a time. Slow and sensual, just how I like it.

His dick stands straight and points right at me. I get on my hands and knees crawling toward him on the bed. My man steps closer and I wrap my short fingers around his long, thick yogurt slinger. He puts his hands behind his head, linking his fingers and leans back as I stroke my tongue gently back and forth up his shaft.

A moan escapes his lips, and I flick my tongue across the head, tasting the glistening pre cum. Pulling away, a strand of it stretches between my mouth and his tip. I look up into his gaze and meet it with blazing heat bursting from my eyes and shove that sucker down my throat hard, making myself gag on the luxurious length of his cock while caressing my tongue up and down. Spit slides down my chin and onto my shirt creating a wet spot. I stop and pull his dick out my mouth with a wet pop.

Sitting up and pulling my shirt off I let my titties free. *No they ain't perky. I'm not fucking twenty. They hang like they have given up on life but so the fuck what.* My man loves them and I can tie them in a knot, I can tie them in a bow. I can throw them over my shoulder...*You're singing it now aren't you?*

He grabs one of my triple D's while the other one just hangs awkwardly. He bites my nipple, and I push him.

"Oh, you want it rough today? Say no mo'."

I lean back on the bed and wiggle out of my shorts and granny panties. I didn't put anything cute on because a bitch got high so he had to deal with the granny panties I wear around the house.

He doesn't say anything but watches me with smoldering eyes while my right hand wraps around his dick as I pull him to the bed.

"Lay the fuck back and let me take this dick."

"My loins are yours, to do with as you please."

I throw my right leg around him, but I'm not facing him, no, this is reverse cowgirl, bitch.

Yeet-haw hoes.

Betchya can't do it like meee!

I grab his dick to adjust it to my opening, sliding it across my clit a few times before slapping my girl, then I slide it in. My pussy is wet-wet. *That's why they used to call me Juice Box.* Wrapping my hands around his legs and laying my face between his knees I bounce my ass up and down on that thang, hard. Working my muscles in one ass cheek and then the other. The sound of my ass clapping as I bounce up and down echo throughout my small bedroom.

"You like this phat ass, don't you, daddy?"

Clenching my cunt then releasing over and over has my boo speaking in tongues. Well, at least it isn't any language I know. Leaning straight up, I keep riding. I can feel my orgasm building up inside of me. I turn a little to the left and it hits my sweet spot perfectly. A few more bounces and I squirt all down my man. I feel it running down the sides of his hips and he grabs my ass cheeks, making me bounce harder, faster with almost inhuman speed.

He makes a weird throaty noise and busts inside of me. I don't mind because I can't have babies anyway, and I love the feeling of us lying there in each other's juices for just a minute. It wouldn't be the same with a condom between us. I trusted my man not to cheat on me so I was secure in having unprotected sex with him. *Ain't my fault y'all bitches always go for the players. Dumb hoes.*

I get up to go take a piss. It's cool to sit for a sec but it ain't like the movies. Those bitches just roll over and go to sleep. Hell to the naw. You better pee first hoe or you gonna get some kinda *yeasta-rhea.* I said what I said. That ain't no typo skank.

I realize I have to poop again as Dorian steps inside my shower. I hesitate then say fuck it. It ain't real love if you can't shit while your man showers. *Shut up bitch, it ain't nasty. I don't stink too bad. It doesn't smell like roses ooh-ooh-ooh, either.*

I take a sip of my latte, I brought in the bathroom with me, and light a Newport to help me poop better.

"My club Hedonia's grand opening is this weekend. Tonight is opening night. I need you there by my side to show the world my beautiful, short, stacked, and sassy lady."

"I ain't no fucking lady. There ain't one damn bone in my body that's lady like." I yell from my throne as a little poop slides out. I shiver because it kinda felt good. *You know what I'm talking about. Don't front, bitches.*

"It's also the unveiling of a new psychedelic I've created, called Lotus. I've been perfecting it with my business associate. Lotus opens the neuro pathways so you can open your mind and let your true inhibitions out. I'm excited to see where the night will take us."

"Sounds like shrooms." I cut him off as I wipe my ass, then flushed.

"Mother of whores!" Dorian shrieks.

"Sorry,I forgot about flushing while you're in the shower. "

Sliding the shower door open, I hop in behind him. He immediately gets out of the way and lets me get to the front, where I can lather my African sponge up and start scrubbing myself. My Vampire Blood, Bath and Body Works shower gel smells amazing, as we are enveloped in the sweet, intoxicating scent of red berries, night-bloom, and jasmine.

"My dear, that smell is my undoing." My love whispers from behind me, and I feel the poke of his reaction against my soapy ass.

"Lemme rinse this shit off first, so it doesn't get all up in my coochie and I get a damn infection," I say playfully, but I mean it. *I don't want soap inside my pussy. That shit burns.*

We have another bang sesh, this time I almost kill myself. He is hitting it from the back, and I slip and hit my damn head on the faucet knobs, bouncing off it and out of the tub.

"Goddamnit"

Dorian picks me up like I don't weigh…..*fuck you bitch, not telling you how much I fucking weigh. Hoe is you for serious?*

He takes me to my room and sets me on my feet, in front of my bed.

"Are you alright my love?" He turned my face up toward his and ran his thumb across my forehead where a welt was already forming. Too bad I don't heal fast like he did. Which was weird in itself but you don't question a good thing. I should have though, I chocked it up to him being Norwegian or whatever. That's what good dick does to a bitch. Makes her ignore all the red flags, waving right in your mother fucking face; but no, you're too dick-whipped to notice or care.

"Yea I'm fine. I'm a fucking warrior princess. I can handle a little bump on the damn head. I ain't no weak bitch, boo."

"You remind me of my old friend Lord Henry Lotto, back in old London. He was as feisty as you, and never backed down."

When he talks like that, old London, etc, Lord, it's weird. He acts like he is over 200 years old. He has never outright said his age but he talks like he is from a different century. Perhaps he used to work at Medieval Times?

"Will you be ok my lovely? I need to get to the club to do some last minute things before we open our doors."

Shaking off my thoughts, I look into his beautiful dark eyes and reply.

"Yes, my big dick daddy with the caaaaandy stick. You might want to put that thing away, or you ain't never making it up out of here!"

He kisses me softly on my lips.

"I am at a loss. I desperately need to get to the club, but looking at your pale flesh, those curves, I do not want to go."

"Awe, boo, you a poetic mother fucker, you know that? Go do yo thang. I'm going to heat up some mozzarella sticks in the air fryer because I need something in my stomach, like now. You took all of my energy. If I'm gonna be able to twerk my thang all up on you tonight, a shorty gonna need to replenish first. I still need to flat iron my hair and do my makeup. You know it takes me forever to get my eyeshadow right."

I'm kinda rambling, so I must still be high. Not high enough, though. Where's my fucking wax?

After Dorian gets dressed, he gives me one more kiss. I accidentally blow the smoke in his face, and he coughs and flaps his hand around trying to fan the smoke.

"My bad. See ya soon." As I start coughing because goddamn that was a huge hit.

My man chuckles and kisses me one last time.

"You need to brush yo teeth, boo. Breath smells like bussy." I say as he leaves.

My phone dings and I grab it but it's just a FB notification. I check my messages and realize I didn't respond to my bitch JJ.

Anyways bitch. There is a new club opening up tonight. How about we meet up and go? You down to shake that bussy? I know I need a damn drink if we're gonna be hashing shit out. Then again can I just say sorry now and that be it?

Please say yes, how

How

Hoe…..urgh

5

Anyhoo, Here's a Meme About Mental Illness

Phrique

I'm in the middle of getting ready to begin preparing to think about starting my homework. Just as soon as I put a few finishing touches on one of the stories I'm working on and Dorian's commission. Then, I'm going into *super-focus mode* on this class that I *totally* care about and am not taking just so I can get an A and be showered with rapidly dissipating validation. Because I am *all* about finishing my degree in a developmental epoch where higher education is basically obsolete, and this is not just a prime example of sunk cost fallacy in real time whatsoever.

I see I have a Facebook notification, and reasoned that my homework would have a better chance tomorrow. Maybe this weekend. I should put it all off until the weekend. That's never bit me in the ass before. Plus it's not like

I had any plans. Yes, this sounded like the absolute best course of action that I wouldn't regret later whatsoever.

Just my luck, the first post on Facebook was the latest horror author getting cancelled for using AI on their newest cover, by authors who still had AI covers in their catalog. After I found twenty-ish posts to drop my books, merch, and/or OnlyFeetz links in, I remembered what I came here for. *A blessed notification!*

Oh, it was just a reminder for Dorian's club opening. I think he mentioned it twenty or thirty times, but if he really wanted me to go, I would think he would just ask me. I mean, I'm not a mind reader, and I HATED passive-aggressive behavior. Which reminded me, *I should text him.*

Not like you care, but I'm alive. It's a good thing you didn't blow up my phone checking on my well-being or anything, because that really would have distracted me. Lucky for you, I was very busy working on your beloved commission, like I promised I would. Because usually when someone CARES about someone else, they keep their promises and act like they give a shit about their interests or that they weren't DEAD IN AN ALLEY SOMEWHERE.

I don't necessarily believe in God or the Devil. However, I do believe that whatever is in charge of punishments on earth has placed you in my life for something TERRIBLE that I've done. I texted you this morning. Twice actually. You never responded; you just sent me a cat meme about mental illness.

My jaw dropped. Who knew the British were such huge liars, innit? I scrolled up skeptically.

~9am
Dorian:

> Good Morning, my scrumptious little caramel brownie, can't wait to see you later.

> Sorry, I forgot. Good morning, I can't see you, but you're looking younger every day. Hopefully I got that right, or I'll be hearing about it for the next week.

Wow. I don't believe it. Was I blatantly wrong about something and had the opportunity to apologize for it? To become a more mature, well-rounded, responsible person and show humility when I didn't necessarily have to?

Then I sent him a meme about how my childhood trauma makes me absolutely hilarious and responded to Asher, finally.

Oh gurl, a clurb? Like a club club? How old are we again? You know what, don't answer that. Yeah, what the hell. #YOLO or whatever the broccoli hair kids say. Do I need to bring a bulletproof vest with me or… cuz this sounds like Club Shady Nasty all over again.

Biiiitch! You know it was called Sha-dynasty and it was lit til they started shooting. No, this shit is going to be high class. Even for your bougie ass. Google it, it's called Club Hedonia. Start picking out your outfit now, cuz you know it'll take a few tries.

Ugh, what was I about to get myself into? What was I going to wear? Did I have a backpack that would match? I walked into my closet, looking at my array of assorted douchebag clothing and hoochie daddy shorts. My phone dings in my hand.

No hoochie daddy shorts, there's a dress code. No backpacks either, we

there to get our drink on, not give a
fashion show bitch!

That is just uncanny. How did she… I forgot how much this bitch knew me so well. Sometimes I forget that even though I'm basically untouchable—a chaotic juggernaut of increasingly intense energy all wrapped up in a jaunty bow—I could be a little extra sometimes. So it's good to keep friends around who get me and don't want me to be anyone but my true self. *Especially since I'm such a refined and complex individual. A fucking delight.*

Ugh, I don't have anything to wear!

Dorian texts me to buzz him in my building. I still can't figure out what I'm going to wear. I'm eying this new hoodie that I haven't been able to show off before. I reason I could make it work, hopefully it wouldn't be too hot in the clurb, girl.

I hear my door open and shut. Dorian sounds like he's on the phone, which is classy and very attractive of him.

Regardless, I step out to greet him. Standing aloofly in his way, he owes me a hug after all. To my shock, he walks past me as he shouts,

"I don't care about testing, I want that shit ready tonight. I have investors breathing down my neck left and right. My name is on the line. Are we understood?"

He stepped out on my balcony to finish his call. Great, give the neighbors more of a reason to stare. Part of me wanted to be nosey, to find out what he means and how that could possibly affect me and my well-being. The other part of me was still stunned that I didn't get any kind of affection. Like who walks past a snack bar and doesn't grab a hand or a mouthful? Or both? Regardless, I was sure this was all his nerves talking so I let him have his little hissy fit. It doesn't happen often, but I can be histrionic sometimes, too. Once in a blue moon. We are human, unfortunately, so it comes with the territory.

When we first met, I had pegged him as a high-strung nerd. He seemed a bit out of place on campus, but then again, so was I. He was a bit older, but not like *old* old. I had to be careful, though; sometimes I forget that ageism

is the most damnable sin known to man. He was coming into the S.T.E.M.building as I was leaving. I accidentally smiled his way. *Finally, someone older than me is out here.* That's what did it, I had accidentally pulled out the charm on some poor innocent. Sorry to this man, who was about to be eating out of the palm of my hand.

"Well, aren't you a most interesting creature?" He said, giving the up-and-down.

I remember this distinctly because he said *creature,* and I wasn't sure if I was supposed to swing on him or not. Then he went with the usual, "Oh, did that one hurt?" question. Pointing to my bridge piercing. I could have pulled out my usual, *nah* and kept it moving, yet some-thing drew me to him. He seemed smart, refined, *clean-* a rare Pokémon spawn indeed, especially out in these parts. So I said, "Not at all." He gave me an incredulous look, which I had anticipated.

"None of them did, really." I add, eye-fucking him with every word. "What's a little pain to make pleasure seem that much more enjoyable?"

Fuck, I winced. That one was bad, even for me, but he cocked an eyebrow, and I knew it was time to reel this one in.

"Besides, beauty is pain. I don't mind it as long as it makes me prettier afterwards."

He smiled and added, "That, it certainly has," with a twinkle in his eye. *Oh, OK, zaddy.*

I apologized if I was keeping him from his class. He said he was just headed to the Bio Lab to see a friend, but would much rather study *me*. That's when I knew I was going to ruin this man's life, and he was going to love every minute of it.

My balcony door shut and locked, knocking me out of one of my claim-to-fame flashbacks. Dorian finally came back in. Now off the phone and ready to make up for his trespasses, I was certain. So certain that I did him a solid and removed my shorts, but kept my boxer briefs on for him. He enjoyed pretending it was Christmas every day. He has enough going on; might as well make his life a little easier, right?

And people have the nerve to call me insufferable.

I'm still cycling through outfits, *alphets* as I like to call them, when he walks in my room and is no doubt awestruck by my package to cake ratio.

"What are you...where are your pants?" He says, looking around the room like I had an entire Brazilian soccer team hiding under my bed. *Red flag, I think he doth project too much. Your honor, please let the record show that I am a slut in theory but never in practice. My toys are limited edition and not for mass consumption.*

"Hello, Earth to JJ," he snaps, his tone already making my tongue slide across my teeth punitively.

"Sorry, dissociating. What's up, sweetcheex? Where am I?" I say, partially joking.

"I don't have time for this. I came by before I headed to Igor's because you said my art was ready," he said, still suspiciously looking around my room.

"Gross. Glad you came here first, otherwise I would have to Lysol you down."

"Can you go a day without antagonizing someone? Not make a snide, unnecessary comment? Be so self-absorbed that you avoid anything not about you at all costs?"

A cherry lollipop magically appeared in my hand. Which I popped in my cheek, while tooching my ass up and I shook everything the Dark Lord endowed me with antagonizingly.

"No*P*e," I said, popping the P.

His handsome face twisted in anger, the ugliest I'd ever seen him look.

However, *I won.*

He all but slapped his palm to his face, trying to calm himself.

"This was a mistake. I should have just called you." He chewed back his angry sneer, "not like you'd pick up anyway."

"Dorian, it's 2025. Your finished commission was emailed to you this morning and updated in our shared folder. As we originally discussed. Completed on opening day. Whatever you've got going on with Stumpy is on you. Don't take that shit out on me."

He blew out an exasperated sigh and swiped through his Jitterbug phone or whatever. I crossed my arms, making them and my mitties look their thickest for this unveiling. This was my best work yet. I knew he was going to love it, forget all the bullshit, and then we could fuck all our aggressions out.

After a few more clicks, his eyebrows furrowed. He used his fingers to pinch zoom, before he scrunched up his face. A miracle occurred, and I actually bit my tongue.

"The body looks great, but-" he squinted to look again. "My face looks horrible! Why is my chin so pointy and my nose so thin?"

"Bitch, I don't know. Ask your colonizing ass ancestors, not me."

Oop. There went my BJ.

"Sorry, your...*don't say inbred, don't say inbred...*regal features were slightly caricaturized, you said I could go a little cartoony with your face. I don't think it looks bad at all, though."

My iPad was charging, so I began to open my connected drawing app on my phone so he could see some of the other looks I had saved when he rudely cut me off.

"I look horrendous. This is the last thing I needed. Can you work on it and get it to me tonight?"

"Bitch, I was going to surprise you and show up tonight, but not if you're going to be a fuckface about all this."

Dorian was physically taken aback. *So dramatic.*

"I asked you how many times? You acted like you wouldn't be caught dead there."

"Well yeah, passive-aggressive digs are my love language. Like, have you met me?"

He clapped his hands together and brought them to his nostrils in thought.

"I don't want you there. You're just going to make it about you and be a diva. I don't need this night ruined by your histrionics."

I chuckled. *This man don't know that I could end him with one look and a string of words.* I looked him up and down and then glanced at the door, for his safety.

"That's it? Is it that easy? No comeback?" he asks, sounding nervous; *deservedly.*

I shake my head and let out a single chuckle before I take off my shirt and go into my bathroom.

He walks out of the room, and seconds later, I hear my front door slam. I let out a huff and shed a tear for my property value as I turned on my shower. I can't believe he is treating me this way, especially acting as if I would make a scene at his precious little club. Well, that settles it. I made up my mind. I could never be a teacher, but I know how to teach a ho a lesson. He'll rue the day he called *me* overdramatic.

Hey girl hey, I'm ready to go when you are. Are we pregaming? Cuz I wanna be EXTRA drunk tonight.

6

This Bitch is Fancier than Applebee's

ASHER

I roll my eyes at JJ's text. Pre-game? Two drinks in and that bitch won't shut the fuck up. His voice gets louder and he has ZERO filter with alcohol in his system. Last time I drank with him he almost got us cancelled in the hallway at AuthorCon. *Not really. Now who's being dramatic?* He did say something that may have turned my face as red as my ass when it's slapped, but it wasn't anything too bad. It was hilarious, just a little too loud. Kinda like him.

> HELLLLL NAW! TO THE NAW NAW NAW. You know we need to pace your ass. Plus I still need to get dressed and I know you will change your outfit ten more times before you leave.

JJ:

How dare you say true things to me about me. FINE. I'll wait till we get there.

Asher:

Give me forty five minutes and I will meet you there. I washed my cunt already but a bitch gotta get high first.

JJ:

I wish I could go back in time & take back whatever I said that would make you think I ever needed to know such details about you, sis.

Asher:

Fuck you hoe

JJ:

Le sigh

Asher:

I love you too, now lemme 'lone

JJ:

ain't got no panties on, on the dance floor meme

I sit my phone down and pick up my dab pen, inhaling that glorious THC. I smoke way more than I should and stare at the wall for ten minutes, thinking about the last episode of Love Island USA.. There was some bullying involved and the whole episode just hit a little too close to home and had me in my feelings.

I think back to the months that I withdrew myself and almost stopped writing. JJ really helped me. I grew so much as a person, and learned the difference between positive friendships and toxic ones. Then me and JJ had a falling out and I almost went right back to my hole. Being able to finally see this hoe tonight is exactly what I need to sidestep that drop.

I finally snapped out of my daydream that made my brain go left when I was supposed to be getting ready. Looking at my wax I giggle to myself. Yeah, maybe I shouldn't be so high when I've got shit to do.

Damn, I'm hungry as fuck though. Thinking of pizza bites I go to my closet and sling it open.

I have no idea what to wear.

An idea pops in my head, and I text my boo thang D.

Asher:

Hey little booty, what are you wearing tonight? I was thinking we could match? Maybe tonight is the night to finally let the pussy out the bag. I'm kinda tired of hiding my man and it's a little suspect tbh.

Dorian:

Oh, my love muffin, I have so much on my plate tonight, let's wait a little longer. I promise, after the club opening and everything is running properly I will, as you kids say these days, "make it official on the gram."

Asher:

Talk like that will make my pussy dry up like a goddamn desert.

SO

FUCKING

CRINGE

Dorian:

My love for you is eternal, but I must parlay. There are still things that must be done.

I roll my eyes. He already gave me that line today. I know he gotta get shit done.

What the fuck ever. He's moving funny all of a sudden.

I pull out my black mini skirt and my favorite long-sleeved black mesh crop top and throw them on the bed. I grab one of my push-up bras that's lying on top of a pile of my clean clothes. I eye the pile like it's my arch nemesis, snatching up a black lace thong. Lastly, I eye my drawer full of fishnets and select a pair.

Once I'm dressed, I look in the mirror. I ogled my own tits and how hot they looked in the black lace. Normally, my tiddies look like they have given up on life, and my nipples forever stare at the fucking floor, but the mesh top fits me like a glove. I put on my shiny combat boots and zip them up the sides before I run to the bathroom to do my makeup.

I'm thinking black eyeshadow, with a tad of white at the top to highlight my eyebrows. It really adds to the look and makes my eyeshadow pop. I swipe a bit of mascara on after I perfect my eyeliner. I dig through my lipsticks until I find my favorite green one. I'm running low, but I pout at myself in the mirror and apply it to my lips anyway.

I actually have a full top and bottom lip unlike how JJ likes to draw me. Hence the cover. I am making an angry face and biting my lip on it but damn ....where my lips go hoe? He already had my face looking like a rectangle. I had to tell that hoe I'm a fat round cheek girl not the fat box face girl. My flat iron heats up in a few minutes, then I fix my short, dyed black hair. For once, I'm happy with how my hair turns out. Then I flip myself off in the mirror, shove my wallet in my tits, and head out.

Dorian's club is in downtown Raleigh and it takes me forever to find a fucking parking spot. I swear it's only the dumbest of drivers on the road tonight. I really hate driving. My hands are always sweaty. The other drivers make me nervous because people can't fucking drive. I'm always thinking that I'll die in a car wreck because of some other idiot.

I had to woo-sa a few times after I almost had to get out of my car and drag a bitch out of hers. This hoe had the audacity to give me the finger after *SHE* cut *ME* off.. I wasn't trying to work up a sweat tussling with some stupid cunt. I finally found a parking spot a block away from the club, so I hoofed it the rest of the way.

The club is a massive two story brick building with spot lights slicing up the night sky above it.

CLUB HEDONIA

is displayed on a huge white LED wall sign. Dorian was sparing no expense. The few exterior windows were blacked out, which added to the mystery for all the FOMO-having shut-ins to balk at. I walk my little ass past a banner under the bright lights that read *When offered pain or pleasure, why not go both ways?* Wow, Dorian was really going all in, huh? A passing thought once I spied the huge fucking line of hoes waiting to get in.

Ain't no way I'm waiting in that when my man's the fucking owner.

I stand off to the side of the line, ignoring the stares and check my messages. I knew this bitch would be late. I hate being late for anything. Hell, if I was on time I would still feel late. I like being early but decided against it this time because I knew my bestie was on C.P. time. (*iykyk.*)

Twenty minutes later, I spotted him behind two ladies in line. One of them—who looks like a younger version of Mariah Carey—gives me an odd look. I ignore it, overwhelmed with the happiness that I feel in this moment and breathe a sigh of relief at seeing JJ again.

It felt like I was stuck in quicksand, spiraling. Then one sight of that harsh judgmental glare—at nothing in particular—and my world is right again. My feet finally feel like they are on solid ground. It's amazing what a good friendship can do.

He looks at the line, flips his hair and rolls his eyes. I can read his mind. *Only the poor wait in line,* or something flippantly catty.

This hoe really pulled out the hoochie daddy shorts. I can't help but smile. Of course they are bright as fuck and match his shoes, socks and ...this mother fucker is wearing a goddamn hoodie! I shake my head and laugh. The most bougie person I know shows up at a fancy club in a fucking hoodie. It's hilarious and to be honest, I expected nothing less.

He saunters up to me with his matching backpack like it's his first day of school. I smell his grape Kool-Aid scented Beetlejuice hair products in the breeze. I wanted to rob him of it at the last con, but then we would have made a scene. I want it but I don't wanna buy it. I want *his.* Sometimes I don't make sense and I'm ok with that.

"So ummmm," his eyes flash from me back to the line.

I don't know how he can cram so much attitude and dramatics into two measly words, but the man is a master at it.

"Yeah, we ain't waiting in that shit. Come on."

I confidently walk past the whispers to the front of the line. The bouncer checking ID's raises his eyebrows at my approach.

"I should be on the VIP list."

"Girl, same. The name is Phrique." JJ pipes up.

"How did you get VIP hoe? And why didn't you mention it when I told you about the club?"

"Baby, if I'm not VIP, I'm not there. Hoes pay me to show up to their lil' shindigs. I bring the party wherever I go."

He delivered that little speech with a totally straight face and the authority that even *I* believed his delusions.

"I see Asher Dark on the list, but nothing about no Freaky."

The large bouncer said monotonously, staring dead ahead, tucking his clipboard back under his arm.

"Hey Frankenstein, look again. It's spelled PHRIQUE." he says, turning to me while not taking his eyes off the bouncer. He loudly whispered, "This Hooked on Phonics mofo. Someone grew up around power lines," under his breath.

I can tell he is getting flustered because he's flipping his hair repeatedly now. The doorman glances at the list again for 1.2 seconds then shakes his head. An array of emotions wash across my friend's face and I can feel him amping up, so before he causes a scene, I yank on the sleeve of his hoody.

"Chill. Don't forget what you always tell me. Too pretty for jail, too pretty for jail."

I clear my throat and raise my voice.

"I should be allowed to have one other person with me, right?" I think I remember hearing that in a movie or something. I don't really *do* clubs. "Yeah" is all the bouncer says. JJ literally has steam coming out of his ears as he furiously taps away on his phone, mouthing each expletive he is texting.

Shew! I would not want to be on the other end of that.

I start to say something because I'm that bitch, but the doorman pipes up.

"No backpacks or hoodies allowed."

Before JJ can end this man's life, I lean in and whisper to the doorman. "I am Dorian Grey's girlfriend. If you don't let me and my friend in right now, there is going to be a big problem."

His mouth opens and closes like a damn fool.

"Just give us the damn VIP bracelets already," I say as I hold my arm out.

He slides a glowing green silicone wristband on my wrist with *Lotus VIP* etched into it. JJ looks mortified that the man might lay his dirty paws on him so he snatches his and slides it on himself.

The bouncer eyes me, then says, "Move it along, ladies," and opens the door for us to enter.

"Smart man," I whisper as we pass him.

JJ gets right in his face. Everyone thinks he's a barking little chihuahua, but he's a tall mofo. I can watch his brain choosing each word wisely as his face knots into a rage. He's pretty, but he can get ugly in a heartbeat.

"You no-business, born-insecure, junkyard-" he paused to collect himself. "From here on out, it's on sight," JJ said through clenched teeth as he pointed two fingers from his eyes to the bouncer's as if to say *I'm watching you.*

Oh, boys, I thought as I finally made it inside this mother fucker. The first thing I notice is all the fucking gold. It's everywhere. It's too much. The walls were gold, the crown molding was fucking gold. They even had clusters of gold shimmering disco balls in clusters scattered in various places to make it look artsy or some shit.

I looked past the entrance at the rows of red booths. Sitting above them is a giant portrait in a shroud, but you can still make out the shape of a man in it. It's encased in inch-thick plexiglass. The bulky gold frame behind it matched the rest of the god awful gold. *Huge, to match his ego.* A gold placard sits below it that simply says

Dorian Gray

To the right of me is a red carpeted stairway and a VIP stanchion written in gold lettering in front of a velvet rope. Another bouncer who looks just like the other one is stationed behind it. My eyes follow the walls lined with oversized golden weapons, hanging above tables and random statues. I would hate to see Dorian's credit card bills.

There's a huge bar toward the center of the club. Dark cherry wood with gold trim wrapping around the support pillars that reach up to the ceiling. Behind the bar sit shelves stocked with every bottle of liquor imaginable. The same dark cherry wood and gold trim matched the booths, tables, and spinning stools. They didn't look comfortable in the slightest. I was going to need a drink before I took in much more of this place. JJ does his grand entrance a full twenty seconds after me, then he does his little stank look around face.

"Whew chillay," he says. I'm glad he said it, not me.

We take in the huge space, wondering what we got ourselves into. JJ is itching to start throwing shade. I can see him making his lists in his head.

Before he could get started, a tall blonde waitress in a gold sequin dress walked up to us. It looked old-timey or *vintage* as fuck. Like something out of the fifties. As a matter of fact, I notice, this whole place has various things from different periods of time scattered about.

The lady had a tray with two bright aqua swirling shots that were in what looked like test tubes. They glow bizarrely, unlike the other drinks everyone else was shooting back.

"The owner sends his apologies for the mix-up at the front door. Please accept these complimentary shots. It's a special elixir we call *"A shot of Immortality."*

She sounded monotone, like she had rehearsed this a hundred times before coming up to us. Am I being paranoid? There was no way she had the time for that. We literally just got in this bitch.

JJ says something that is drowned out by the sound of feedback from one of the giant speakers, so I miss it.

We grab our shots and seats at the bar. I throw mine back while JJ looks at it skeptically for a minute before sniffing it. Then he tosses it back, making a face. *Lightweight.*

"Well, at least we finally made it in. About time I saw your ass again." I say, hoping he wasn't still feeling froggy.

"Yeah, all that was so shitty. We knew better. I think I just let so much get to me, plus I was finishing up a story, and you know I'm kinda learning that I go in ghost-mode when I'm hunkering down." He sounded sincere, *that shot must be kicking in,* I thought with a chuckle.

"Well it was worth it, you know I loved *Scissor Me Timbers.* I'll never look at a pie or a nun the same ever again."

JJ tossed his head back and laughed. He still didn't realize how much he flipped his gotdamned hair. Maybe he will after all this.

"Girl, I'm so burnt out. I definitely needed a break after all that. I don't want to see a drag queen or a nun for a long ass time."

Like clockwork, as soon as he said that, two suspiciously large women walked past us. One decked out head to toe in a vinyl nun's habit. The other one rocked a glitter beard and a Mariska Hargitay wig. I gave them a snap for their looks while JJ slammed his head down in his arms on the bar top.

"I hate it here." He muffled, as I held in my chuckle.

"Like here? Or?" I said, going down the walls with my eyes to see how many golden weapons I could remember the name of.

"Like this planet." He said, popping his head back up.

I snickered. I love him to death, but he's so much more entertaining when he has one of his hourly crises.

"This bitch is fancier than Applebee's, that's fo sho."

"Applebee's ain't fancy. Your hillbilly is showing, sis." JJ responds as he stares up at a disco ball as big as a grand piano.

"What's with all the gold?" I say.

"What is this trash ass music?" he says stankily.

"At least the bar looks stocked." I say, "I've never seen so many shiny disco balls." I say, letting out a little giggle. That shot was kicking in.

"How is *Lucifur* coming along?" he asks.

"It's getting there. I'm a few chapters in, but I can't wait to see where it goes. I love it so much."

Just then, a barrage of lasers slice through the smoky air, illuminating the ceiling, sending fractals through the disco balls.

"Enough fucking lasers!" JJ yells loudly as they light up his face. An extra bright blue laser ricochets off the gold mace on the wall across from us and beams right into JJ's fake purple contact. He dramatically howls like he's been shot, and I practically have to hold him upright.

"Are you OK?" I ask, thinking my friend just got LASIK *again*.

"That motherfuckin D-" he stammers, holding his teary eye. "Wait till I sober up and get on the horn with my lawyer; they might as well sign the deed over to me now." He says, reaching over the bar to grab some napkins. I roll my eyes, *bless his heart, he's so dramatic.*

"Histrionic Personality Disorder! Look it up, bitch! It's no cakewalk for me, either."

Wait, how did he?

His eye is still tearing up.

"I need to rinse my eye out, my shit is burning," he says. "Watch my bag, will you?" He asks, already walking away.

"Ok Xtra Mayonessa," I snicker as he turns back toward me and gives me the "alright ho, you got me there" face. I watch him walk into the hall along the back, under a *Restrooms* sign. This mother fucker is organized, I'll give them that. Further down the line, I see another sign for an *Outside Patio.*

I dig in my titties for my cigarettes. *Don't mind if I do.*

I walk across the dance floor, making my way outside. A giant disco ball hangs from the center of a glass-tinted ceiling. The tint was darker than the tint on my car windows, making it impossible to see through.

Next to the Patio door is a gold statue of a minotaur. Not sure how I missed that before. The mythological Greek creature looked right out of a textbook, with the head of a bull and the body of a man. Hooves hold up his massive frame. Holding an axe raised in his right hand, he wards off would-be foes with his left hand. I'm kinda mesmerized as I get closer. The arms on this thing are bigger than any bodybuilder I'd ever laid eyes on. It's buck-ass-naked, and his giant member hangs well to his knees. Makes me kind of understand all those monster fucker books. I mean, the thing could destroy my uterus, and I would probably let it. What the fuck is wrong with me? Is this what JJ refers to as *the vapors*? My eyes land on his massive horns. They look like they could eviscerate me with no hesitation. The fuck am I thinking? Sometimes I'm just a horny hoe, I guess.

Please be okay, JJ, The last thing the world needs is for you to actually get hurt. We'd never hear the end of it.

I giggle to myself as I step outside and find the patio is pretty empty. Just a couple talking and another statue. I recognize this one as a Lamia. She has a beautiful woman's upper body, but her lower half forms a giant snake tail, wound up in a tight twist. Its golden scales reflecting the moonlight make sparkles dance along the walls.

Finishing my cigarette, I'm about to text JJ. I know he is just going to the bathroom, but that could take forever. He might stop in front of the mirror and admire himself or fiddle with his hair like it couldn't get any more perfect than it already was. I lug his big ass backpack on my little ass body and decide to check out the VIP room before it gets too packed.

Before I even have time to get nervous about approaching security or can even say anything, he unlatches the velvet rope and holds it aside for me. I begin my walk up the red carpeted stairs that lead to the second story.

As I reach the top of the stairs, I am greeted by a huge room that's just as gold and blinding as the main floor. Thankfully, this spot is free of those god-awful-lasers.

My eyes darted to the giant gold statue of a griffin in the center. While plush red couches wrap around the entire space. They're the same red as the carpet on the stairs, but there's no carpet up here. *It's a see-through floor. You can see the whole club from up here.* People are dancing and gyrating on each other, oblivious that we can see their every move. I watch as the entire crowd moves in one glorious rhythm. It made me want to get out there and be sucked into a mass of wiggling bodies.

Where the fuck is JJ?! I want to pop my pussy!

I'm about to go and find his ass when I get a little woozy. It must be the glass. I was getting a little nervous. I fucking hate heights. I'm only five feet tall. I ain't meant to see this high up. Thank Satan, the glass looks sturdy, and I wore panties today.

The couches are lined with comfy-looking, lush pillows. My head is spinning, so I head over to one for a pit stop. I drop the heavy backpack beside me. *Seriously, what the fuck does he keep in this thing?*

I think that shot had a little extra umph in it. Jesus what is that shit? 100 proof? Warn a bitch next time.

The pictures that line the walls are of men and women from different centuries. All of them have an aristocratic look of high society brats. JJ would fit in perfectly up here, with his regal ass.

Ugh, I need to get up because baby, the room is a-spinning. Shew. I ain't no lightweight but goddamn.

Standing up, I wobble a little bit before I can regain my balance.

Yeah, I need to find JJ.

I check my phone. I've been up here way too long. As I'm leaving VIP, I notice another woman leaving as well. Something about her face bothers me. Her nose is pointed, almost like a beak. I shiver when I realize what's bothering me about her. She looks like a bird. I hate birds. They fucking terrify me. I have this nightmare where a bird pokes my eyes out and eats them, then laughs at me as I scramble around on the floor searching to get away from the murderous thing.

Another nightmare flashes in my mind, and I immediately push it away. *I will not think about that one.*

I go back downstairs to find my friend. Please let this night get better. I've got a bad feeling about this place.

7

The Clownery, Your Honor

PHRIQUE

My head was a swirl of anger, confusion, and pretty colors. *More than usual.* This time it was way worse, though, and I hate being dramatic. All my nerve endings felt fuzzy. My thousand thoughts a minute slowed to only a few hundred a minute crawl. I know I was in danger, girl. The faces of the clubgoers around me transformed from jovial mouth-breathers and gap-toothed bar wenches to shadow creatures that terrorized me for totally different reasons. My eye wouldn't stop tearing up. Maybe I would feel better if I got away from this tacky pop-trance-shit that I could feel thumping through my chest cavity.

The low light of the hall that led to the bathroom didn't do my already overactive imagination any favors, but I pressed through 'til I made it to the hopefully-not-too-dingy restroom, pushing through the door on wobbly legs and meandering to the sink. The fluorescent bulbs flickered above me. I stood under whichever one seemed to be working and attempted to rinse out my eye. Of course, the faucet groaned and thrummed, but no water came out whatsoever. Luckily, my vision was blinking back to normal. I guess I won't be suing my man after all, but he still needs to get this shit fixed. *What is he running here? A no-tell-motel?*

Pulling out my phone, about to text his ass when I noticed how hard it was to read anything on my screen. In the distance, I hear the click of heels approaching just before the door bursts open. In walks the sinister, yet sickening drag queen nun from before. Under the strobing fluorescents, she glanced in my direction and paid me dust. Er, I mean, she <u>disregarded me as a human and looked at me like I was an ant quivering below her platform heels</u>. *I forget not everyone is familiar with 'The Breeder Glossary' from my beloved "Gig of the Damned: Slay the Competition."* Out of habit, I say,

"Signed copies available on my BigCartel," mortified at my own outburst.

The drag queen is already demurely relieving herself in the urinal when she snaps her head to the side and says,

"Yeah, there is a big fart smell in here," before she shakes off and walks toward the sinks.

I make a confused face as I'm still addle-mindedly swiping on my phone. She finds out the faucets don't work as well.

"Oh yeah, sorry girl," I say, "I should have warned you."

Beyond frustrated, I jam my phone back in my pocket and take my leave. I do my best to smile in her direction and give her a head nod. She glares at me through the mirror's reflection, lipstick still in hand.

"Wait a damned minute, Mary," she spat. "Aren't you that *prick* that killed a bunch of drag queens and wrote about it?"

She drops her lipstick back in her clutch and turns to face me. I put my hands up in defense, not knowing what she could be packing in that change purse.

"So first off, it's pronounced *freak*. I don't know if it's like a public school thing or what, but phonics is a thing and I can only correct people so much."

"Oh, so now you're saying drag queens are dumb too? You wanna come for the doll babies? Kill my good Judies and then write some little book about it? With that lesbian haircut? Do you have no scruples whatsoever?"

The air siphoned from my lungs like a pierced balloon. I reeled from the barrage of slights, hemorrhaging like a mortal wound to my ego.

"I'll have you know, gentle-heifer, that my lil' book is 6x9 and is critically acclaimed."

"I heard *Woom* was better."

I gasped with the strength of a thousand abuelas, feeling my lungs ache with disgusted over-exaggeration. I got close enough to clock her immaculately blended eyeshadow, her razor-sharp cat eye, and even her well-trimmed beard-chest hair combo. Then my painfully-observant eyes trained on her unblended hairline, and I knew I struck gay gold. I couldn't stop staring at the glaring flaw as I fired back,

"YOUR LACE IS SHOWING MUH-MAW!"

With a dainty flourish, her blue-collared man-hand collided against the side of my cherubic cheek. Her open palm left a red welt as well as the sobering sting to match. I recovered from her audacity and the blow before I launched at her with a barreling shoulder to her big-backed torso.

"How many times do I have to tell you bitches! Not the motherfucking face!" I screamed, shockwaves reverberating through the rank space.

The vexed vamp's snatched body flew back, while her chunky heels struggled to keep her upright as she teetered into the open stall. The door swung back, slamming shut as I heard her shuffling behind it.

I quickly turned to check my face in the mirror. The mug was a little red. Well, terra cotta, but no harm done. I blew my reflection a dizzy little kiss and turned to this tempestuous tunic-turnt testament to turpitude. Then it hit me. *That amazing alliteration AND a throwback, as well as the fact that I may or may not have just committed a hate crime. Against one of my own. Could you imagine the bad press? My PR rep would be furious, and good luck ever getting brunch reservations in this town again.*

"Hey girl, hey," I said nervously, "Is you...okurrr?"

The sound of scraping metal sliced through the air from inside the quaking stall. I felt an odd pressure behind my eyes, and my vision seemed to have cut out for a few seconds before the drag queen's sonorous voice resounded above the scrapes.

"This is all a joke to you, isn't it?" rang out from behind the door.

It sounded darker, bassier, like I really let her have it, apparently.

"We are just characters in your little books and material for you to spew the same *tired* schtick about?"

I step closer to her enclosed fortress, growing nervous as the stagnant air feels heavier. The flickering lights ceased to a dull glow.

"98% of what I say is jokes, booboo. It's all part of the brand. I'm flippant, irreverent, sardonic, and a big fan of $10 words. It's all a trauma-response, I'm pretty sure. I haven't really unpacked all that yet. How much time do you have?"

"Not enough time in the world," an angry, demonic voice answers back. "The brand this, the brand that. You know what the brand really is? When you go deep down and find the little boy cowering behind it," it threatens.

"No!" I shriek, pounding on the door, "Please don't! I can't handle constructive criticism, and I will secretly hold it against you until the day you hit the dirt!" I sniffle. "And I'm doing my best to keep this novella-length! I swore!"

A hoot straight from the depths of hell resounds as the light flickers brighter, showing huge swathes of fabric cascading from below the stall.

"Good luck with that."

The sound of slicing comes through the powder-coated steel as long pink claws protrude from the deep cuts. I back away in fear. My back hits the door, I scramble to open it, but find no handle or pull whatsoever.

I nervously laugh, "Girl not dis!" as the lights go out completely.

"What's so funny FREAK?" echoes through the pitch blackness. "Are we funny? Are we entertaining to you? Here to amuse you?" the thousand voices screeched, shredding my ear drums.

The metal squeaking and tearing resonated louder, before the dead silence.

"LIKE A ... CLOWN?"

The words ripple through me as the lights miraculously flood the space and the menacing monstrosity erupts from her ammonious den. Slivers of thin, sharp metal fly in all directions like tangy shrapnel. They cause the wall-length mirror over the sinks to rain down shards of glass like a waterfall of glittering ferocity. A ninja-star-shaped hunk pinwheeled past my face and thunked deep in the hardwood door. I slink to get away from it and scream like a manly, yet appropriately-piped little girl. Staring back at me is an amalgamation of polkadot fabric with wild, undulating aberrations jerking and crackling beneath it. A pandemonium of honking horns and nightmarish giggles harpoons my eardrums, like the fanfare of hell itself.

From within the circus tent of spotted fabric emerged cartoonishly large white gloved hands. Each set erupts from the polka-dots and continues to grow from large stalk-like forearms until they almost scrape the ceiling. After a small forest of them sprouted, the crest of Mount Clownery began to swell and shake. To my horror, a head erupts from within the immense folds, born of my torment and suffering. Its face was bone white, emaciated with a large, overdrawn mouth that housed what seemed like thousands of sharp, needle-like teeth. Its nose was a gnarled red orb that resembled the planet Mars, leaking thick, phlegmy mucus that pooled on the floor beneath it.

I won't even get on the hair, because we've already established what a mess it already was. However, when I looked into its eyes, its soulless black- eyes, I almost lost it. Through the black shine of the onyx spheres, I could see galaxies far away. Black holes that housed truths that would tear the human mind to bubble gum pink confetti. Even my complex and highly esteemed think-piece could not fathom what was beyond the dark depths. It was as if my brain knew just what would make it self-destruct and my bladder release, all rolled into a nightmare that I couldn't awaken from.

My face was awash with horror at this *actual* abomination; my mind reeled. Then the life bar flashed above its head and took up almost the entire expanse of my vision.

I loudly whispered, "Biiiiiiitch," and prepared myself for my first *actual* boss battle.

I side-step the spiky protuberance from the door, trying to utilize the fundamental opening scene that they give all characters at the beginning of the boss fight. *Hands flying, teeth gnashing, acidic flying pies perhaps?*

The door handles are still missing, so I kick at the oversized ninja star, letting it clatter to the floor. A sliver of light pours into the sparsely lit space. As expected, I see the cartoonish hands grow lengthy claws and begin their cycle flying in my direction. I duck the first swipe and grab the metal projectile. Aiming for its dome piece, the sharp metal thunks into the deformed diva's monstrous forehead, spraying buckets of cruor in all directions. Its life meter drops to 66% and I utilize the moment to perform the only super move I can think of.

I jam my face up against the cavernous hole in the door (pause) and scream at the top of my lungs.

"White woman in danger! HELP! There are immigrants in here minding their business and attempting to steal the American dream! Send help before they run a train on me!"

I fear the loud trash music has drowned out my best Ashleigh impression, but before I can try again, I hear the unmistakable sound of soaring clown claws. Three clown hands slam against the wall in front of me, blocking the only other hope I have for escape–the window. I can see the clown-bomination gearing up for another attack, so I have no other choice but to traverse below the long, extended arms. The razor-sharp talons just miss me as I dive, sliding more than I had hoped on the disgustingly damp tile.

"Peepee!" I shriek, "Peepee!" as I army-crawl through.

I do my best to avoid the broken mirror pieces, but the shards are scattered everywhere on this mistaken path. I begrudgingly roll closer to the heavy-breathing beast, feeling more urine and floor-dirt-tea soak into my hoodie. I try to calm my screams and not alert the monster to my whereabouts, but my ick-factor has taken over. I hop up on the other side and shudder in disgust. I let out a revolting howl I didn't know I was holding.

The creature pulls its limbs back inside itself, and a deep laugh erupts from what sounds like leagues below it. It waits for me to express my final airless scream to add,

"But Phrique! You -"

I suck in a quick breath and belly ache more, feeling the disgusting liquid soaking in and beginning to touch my skin. I hold back tears, summoning my mental fortitude to kick in at *any* time now. My breath catches in my throat, allowing the monstrosity to continue.

"But Phrique! You like ho-"

"I loved this hoodie!" I yell out, "I didn't even get to take a selfie in it yet!"

I can feel those abysmal eyes glaring at me as I acquiesce and look for any kind of weapon I can get my hands on.

"But Phrique!"

The cacophony of damned souls pauses, but I yield while I ball up the sleeve of my *ruined* hoodie and pick up the biggest mirror shard I can find.

"I thought you liked horror!" it states matter-of-factly, eager for my irked response.

I don't hear it because I'm too busy using the inside of this soon-to-be-incinerated hoodie to wipe something gross off my face. *I just pissed it off now.*

With a final hasty swipe at my face, some schmutz gets in my mouth. I spit and silently scream while a blinding light glows above me. I feel all my senses go into hyperdrive as I try to find its source. It seems to evade me every time I try to look up, but I see it glinting in the mirror shard's reflection. A charging meter shines above my head. I fight to make out the word above it with my trembling hands. That's when my ADHD goes into hyperfocus and the word RAGE flashes in red above. Every hair on my body stands on end as I turn toward my homicidal, ferociously, flamboyant foe.

Its arduous appendages reemerged from its mass. The claws float above its ailing body, but they looked longer and more threatening. Even in my enraged state, a trickle of sweat crept down my tensed spine. The hot pink hand closest to me started to glow ominously before it rocketed toward me. I side-step the attack, but catch the still glowing palm with a well-timed downward stab of the mirror shard. Its life meter drops a notch, and the creature lets out an angry wail.

"RUDE!" it screamed.

The injured claw dropped, lifeless, on the cold, wet floor. Its other hands flashed, leading my eye to the same glow coming from its cloaked center.

I smile a knowing smile, look at the *nonexistent camera*, and give it a wink. Any gamer nerd worth his weight in Mountain Dew knew a sign from the Poke'gods when he saw one. The rage meter above my head turned blood red, and I felt the glass shard in my hand buzzing.

In that moment, all the built-up rage I had amassed, from losing the 3rd grade spelling bee to catching every Drag Race season finale spoiler at first log-in, consumed me. My motions became synchronized blurs as I artfully stabbed each open palm. Blood spurted from them, like exploded jugs of Hawaiian Punch as I tootsie-foot-ed upon the convulsing, roaring clown. Both our eyes metronoming from my improvised blade to its vulnerable belly. Its life meter flashed with a measly sliver of energy. I bring the shard above me and change my grip as the last of my rage meter dwindles.

A wounded claw clamps onto my arm just as I begin to guide its final descent to end this clownery once and for all. The makeshift blade slowly continues to lower as I strain using the last of my rage.

With a final exhausted breath, I utter

"This hoodie...was a limited edition."

Its black eyes flicker, becoming human for a second before it roars back *halitosisially,*

"Write a book about it."

It lets out a pained whimper as the shard plunges deep into the polka-dotted pile. The nightmare creature roars loud enough to make my ears ring as its life meter flashes its final notches. Warm blood coats my hand, but not enough for my waning rage. I piston my arm, jooging the last sliver of life from this ha-ha-ho's meter. A torrent of inky-black gore blasts my victorious body across the room. I bounce off the damaged wall, catching the side of my head on the sink. My body finally came to a standstill, splayed out on the filthy, blackening floor. My arms in snow angel formation in the darkening depths.

8

You Ride That Mother Fucker?

Asher

I get to the bar and of course JJ is nowhere in sight. Lordt! This man better not be in the bathroom getting his PHRIQUE on. Nah, he would never. That bitch is too bougie for a bathroom bust-it-down. I mean, I think so, but his hoochie daddy shorts kinda say otherwise.

This place is starting to get packed. A sense of panic is rising in me. The walls feel like they're closing in. It's been a while since I've been out in public, so I can get overstimulated pretty easily. Hell, the decor in this place almost made me turn away and go the fuck home.

I don't like being around a lot of people, not anymore. I start to hear my heartbeat speeding up in my ears. I wish JJ would fucking hurry, because standing in a loud, huge club full of people, I feel so fucking alone. I try not to let this feeling consume me. I remember to breathe. *Breathe Asher, or else you're going to be balled up on the bathroom floor, going through one of your many panic attacks while your blood pressure skyrockets.* I need to sit down. A line from one of my favorite movies pops into my mind,

"*I'm feeling a little woozy here.*"

I eye the barstool, wondering if I really want to try and hop my ass up there, but I don't know if I can do it without help. I damn sure ain't asking none of these hoes here. Damnit JJ! He's handy sometimes, when he's here, that is. *Hoodie-wearing backpack-toting bitch.* Oh shit! I reach for my shoulder, searching for the backpack strap, already knowing I don't feel its weight on my back.

Fuck! I must have left it up in the VIP section. Goddamn that shit got me all fucked up in the Clurb. I let out a huge sigh. I don't want to go up those damn steps again (I got short legs and a lot of ass, and get tired quickly) and trudge back down. *Too bad bitch, you know he would kill you if that shit came up missing. We're on a cease-fire mission, remember?*

I make it up the staircase holding in little coughs and look around. There are a lot more people up here than before. *How the fuck? I was literally just up in this bitch.* Ugh. I spot JJ's flashy metallic backpack and immediately thank Daddy Satan that I don't have to fight with this hoe over a lost bag. I don't know why he even brought it, let alone left it with me. I don't even use a pocketbook most of the time. *Plus, I'm old as hell, and still call it a pocketbook.* I just shove everything in my tits. *Bing, bam, boom. I'm not leaving these fun-bags anywhere. No bags forgotten, no tiddies left behind.* I prepare myself and sling this big ass bag over my shoulder, but the weight makes me spin and run right into someone.

"Excuse you motherfucker" I say to the asshole that is all up on my ass.

I look up and into the face of an *avianesque* woman. *Avianesque, wow, I've been hanging out with JJ for too long. That shit must be contagious- Anyways, back to the bird beak bitch.*

She is a little too close for comfort. Her eyes are dark. Her pupils are unrecognizable. There's an eerie silence between us, as she gives me a hawk-like stare, like she's about to scoop up a hunted field mouse.

Well I ain't Fievel, bitch.

I push her ass back some, standing my *lower* ground; because who the fuck does Tweetytwat think she is?

The skanky sparrow barely moves. Goddamn, I think, winded. She is solid as a wall. I'm about to step around her when she opens her mouth and *squawks* at me. I said *biiiiiiiitch.* To my horror, her mouth has extended into a beak. Little baby white feathers begin to sprout up between her eyes and down her jawline. I can't believe what I'm witnessing, as the harpy spreads her arms out. Not arms, but wings! Giant ass mother fucking wings. In an instant, she has turned into some kind of bird-woman.

It's the scariest thing I've ever seen in my whole *some-thing-something* years on this earth.

The motherclucker lunges, but I move before her beak stabs the air where my face was. *This harpacious hoe is trying to kill me!*

Fear be damned, I pull my arm back and release my fist into her lower jaw -or beak- or whatever. Her birdie head snaps back like a Big Bird Pez dispenser, with the force of my blow. *Don't let the fact that I need a stepstool to get into most trucks fool you; I ain't no weak hoe. I boxed for years. Fuck around and find out what these hands do.*

I punch the creature two more times before she can right herself from the first blow.

Some people have superpowers. JJ says his mutant power is revenge. Fighting was one of mine.

Blood spurts from her cracked mandible. She painfully opens it to screech in my face, making my gotdamned ears ring, smacking me across the face with her right wing. My head snaps back, and I taste my own blood.

"Nah, nah. You do not want to go blow for blow with me, Cunt-a-too!"

She glares at me before she spreads her wings and takes flight. I ball up my fists, trying to find a way to avoid being pecked to death. I run for cover under the closest thing, the big ass Griffin. I'm running as fast as my little baby legs can carry me when she swoops down. I feel a searing pain as her bill stabs through my calf, tearing through fishnet and flesh.

"You flapping whore." I scream.

Pain radiates from the nasty, jagged gash, making my butthole tighten. Before she can take off again, I turn in place and roundhouse the bitch in the face just as she makes another jab at me. My leg is throbbing now. I see her fly back up after my boot connects, then I scramble under the gold statue as quickly as I can.

Meanwhile, our little bird and cat fight has caused the crowded VIP lounge to panic. There's a damn stampede to get out! People are trying to bypass others, blocking the door, and now everyone's clogged in one spot. The feather-covered fuckface tries to grab me from under the Griffin, but she can't reach. She is mad as a woodpecker on a steel pole. She takes her anger out on the poor suckers stuck in place, who can't seem to understand that if they would just walk single file, they could all fit down the stairs to escape—but people are stupid and they prove that time and time again. *That's why I like dogs better. Where was I? Oh yeah, bird bitch.*

So the nasty nestwarmer dives into the crowd, slashing and tearing at any flesh its beak can reach. Lunging at a screaming woman, it jabs its pointy beak in her eye, pulling it out of the socket. I watch, mortified, as it squishes the eyeball between its mighty mandible and swallows. I'm stuck to the spot, wanting to help but knowing that I can't do shit. I pause, frozen in fear, before I smack myself back to *reality*. My heart was beating a mile a minute. Please don't let me have a heart attack right here, or a fucking stroke. Talk about being over-god-damn-stimulated now.

Fuck, the room is spinning.

I slap myself again, hard as fuck.

Get it together hoe, we gotta get the fuck outta here.

A severed arm flies through the air and lands right beside the statue.

Jesus, it's literally tearing those poor people to pieces.

The floor under me begins to shake. I look up as the statue ripples like water before it comes alive.

"What the fuck?" I holler as I roll out from under it and get to my feet. *So it may or may not have taken me two tries to get to my feet. I won't talk about my old creaky knees or your mama's, deal?*

The Griffin shakes out his luxurious mane, turning its head toward me. It looks at me square in the eye, and I almost shit my pants. There may have been a little bit of a prairie dog moment, but it went back in.

The griffin spreads its massive wings and roars in my face, blowing my hair back and soaking me with spittle. *Fucking ew! Also, bitch, chew some gum. Stanky Mc-Stank breath ass. Jeebus.*

It takes a mighty swipe at me, its razor-sharp claws extended. I jump up onto the couch before it can dissect me mid-air. I grab one of the many portraits off the wall and frisbee it at the griffin, but it swats it away like a bothersome gnat. About two cushions down from the one I'm standing on, I spot a gold sword next to another bougie ass painting that gleams like it was singing my name. *Aaaaaaasherrrr, come kill a bird bitch with meeeee!*

I jump trampoline style and bounce–like a cartoon character–grabbing the gleaming sword off the wall, just as the shifting bird bitch decides she is done with tearing apart the others. This hoe wants to finish the job she started and comes flying at me.

In one swift move, I jump off the cushion into the air–sword raised like I'm goddamned Xena Warrior Princess–and cut the harpy's head off in one clean slice. Blood arcs above her, showering us in warm splatters of victory. I feel like mother fucking Spartacus. Watching her head– now returned human–drop to the floor and roll toward my boot. Her eyes remain birdlike. I shiver, pushing the dread away, to flex my foot and kick it across the room.

The Griffin lets out a deafening screech, shaking the already panicked room. I clamp my hand over my ears as the beast starts fucking up the room like a toddler throwing a fit. It rips pictures off the walls, sending a handful of VIP's dropping in pained screams for reasons unknown. His big ass starts tearing through the upholstery, tossing cotton everywhere, coming my way.

After a moment or two of throwing a tantrum, he turns to me and narrows his eyes in my direction. The world slows down as if it's me and the monster in the center of the calm storm. All the noise sucked out, nothing moving. Behind us, utter chaos still runs rampant through the crowd, but nothing else matters but him and I at this moment. It's just us facing off like gladiators. *How do I know the giant lion-bird is a he? Well I can't really ask him his pronouns right now–but I can't help but notice a huge feathery dick flopping–so I'm just gonna assume on this one. Just this once, though.*

He rears up on his hind legs, bringing his front two talons down hard on the glass floor. I hear glass crackling. He slams down three more times until I watch a spider-web of cracks spreading out like the sun's rays, and the floor beneath us all shatters.

The survivors and I scream in slow motion. Even the goddam griffin screams, albeit his out of anger, ours because we are all about to fall to our painful deaths. *Duh.*

The Griffin takes flight, just as the floor shatters beneath us. I grab onto one of the beams that supports the glass floor-ceiling and hang like my life depends on it, because it did, bitch*! I couldn't believe this was how my life was about to end. Just my luck, it would be raining clean tiddies and I would still catch a dirty dick.*

My grip lasted a whole three seconds.

You see, I don't have good upper-body strength. I got a big head and little arms, like a T-Rex. JJ hides things on top shelves from me and laughs because I never get any of the good cereals at the store.

My whole body straining, I let go. I kissed it down to Satan, accepting my fate. Luckily, Underworld Daddy was listening, and I miraculously landed on the big feathery beast's back.

Yeet-haw mother fuckers & hail Satan!

Kevin Heart's voice instantly pops into my head, and I hear "*You ride that mother fucker?*"

We swooped around the club, bodies falling all around us, when I chanced a glance down and witnessed a man snap his spine on the bar as he landed with a sickening crunch. Another body falls on a jagged, upturned piece of glass that cleaves through his body, leaving behind two steaming halves. A redheaded femme's body collided with a husband, who had been dancing with his wife when the bodies started to drop. The wife screams at the sight of her husband sprawled out on the floor, neck bent and broken bones stabbing through the bleeding woman lying on top of him.

Chaos ensues as people try to take shelter from any more falling bodies. My monstrous ride has had it with my stowaway ass. It bucks like a bull, which sends me flying to the piles of screaming bodies and broken glass below. My final thought- *I would definitely have been a terrible rodeo rider.*

Then, like a thunderclap, I land on my ass right on the stool at the bar I had been eyeing earlier. JJ's bag is in my lap. I look around with wide eyes and sweat dotting my brow. Everything seems normal. No broken glass. No dead bodies. My eyes shoot up above the crowded, loud club to stare into the intact ceiling and my reflection. The screams have silenced. Everyone is dancing and grooving, making the most of their lives, like they're gonna die young.

Ugh.

I stare down at the cut on my leg in disbelief, the only evidence that I just had to fight for my life. Suddenly, a golden feather drifts down and lands in front of me on the bar; before the bartender wipes it away and gives me a wink.

Man, fuck all this. I did not just pull an "it was all a dream?"

Where the fuck is Dorian at? He should have made his presence known by now. How dare he ignore me on his big night? And where the fuck is JJ? His ass is probably picking his perfect teeth with some twink right now.

You know what, I need a Newport. I pull my cigarettes and lighter out of my tiddies, then waddle my way towards the smoking area sign I spotted earlier. Fuck, maybe I needed some fresh air too. *If this - bitch ain't at the bar by then, WELP. I'll go in that bathroom after his ass. It's nothing I haven't seen before. Dicks out or not, IDGAF. Shit is getting weird around this mother fucker.*

9

Cover Your Fucking Mouth

Phrique

"What in the actual fuck?! All this for some trade?! Wake your ass up, JJ!"

Asher's soothing, husky drawl forced my eyes open. To my sheer horror, I'm staring up at my very concerned friend and a dirty-looking ceiling. I shriek and sit up abruptly, clutching my dampened chest.

"ERNEST?! I'M IN THE MORGUE!"

Asher frustratedly grabs at my arm, pulling me up off the filthy bathroom floor as she's looking around at the trashed restroom.

"The filthy bathroom floor?! What the fuck are they putting in these Applebee's ass drinks?!" I yell out with the appropriate amount of histrionics.

A shrill scrape comes out of the corner stall before the entire enclosure falls in on itself. I attempt to wash my hands as we both watch it cautiously before we scuttle out into the darkened hallway again.

The new wave-synthpop-funk-step bullshit is making my head throb more as I'm trying to piece together what the hell just happened. Asher hits me in the shoulder with the back of her hand.

"Bitch did you get gay bashed? You can tell me. I'll fuck them up."

I scoff.

"Bitch, I wish a motherfucker would try it," I say, pulling my soiled hoodie off and forlornly looking at it as I set it on a barstool.

"Besides, this is a bisexual club. Who's gonna gay bash me? The one guy not wearing leather pants?"

She chuckles, softening her rigid body language, finally.

"Well, there's some weird shit going on in here. I don't feel right. Maybe there's a gas leak or something."

I motioned to the bartender for a drink. He scowls at me when I mouth, *in a clean glass, please* and smile.

"Water! Get him a water!" she interjects rudely & *unsouthernly.*

She looks behind me and around the club before she grabs her phone and begins to text angrily.

"Oh yeah, thank you for inviting me out by the way. I was starting to become a hermit between drawing, writing, and getting d–" I pause when I see her typing like a mad woman.

"Please don't update Facebook about this. It's not my finest moment." I say as the bartender stankily hands me a water bottle.

I press it to my forehead, hoping it will calm what feels like the beginning of a punkass migraine.

"I'm not. I'm texting my man to find out what the hell kind of joint he is running here" She says angrily.

"Your man?" I say, watching the dancefloor from below the condensation-dripping bottle.

"Yeah, I'm dating the owner." She says, finishing her text before she shifts closer to the bar and orders herself a drink. I follow her with my eyes inquisitively, trying to drown out the deafening music.

"You must mean you're dating his skuzzy drug fiend partner or whatever. *I'm* dating the owner."

I say, concern telling me to put the water down, as she turns with a tequila sunrise in hand. I watch her lips move from her drink as she begins to speak at the same time as me. The loud music made us both shout just as the *song* came to a hushed lull.

"I'm dating Dorian!" we both yelled, matter-of-factly, before it registered to both of us.

Her eyes narrowed. So did mine. Her mouth pulled tight into a sneer. My lips puckered in contemplation. We both glare at each other, neither of us willing to break the silence.

"OMG, *SO* Meta!" a gay, disembodied voice yelled out from the dancefloor.

"You must mean another Dorian." She says, stepping closer to me, eyeing me distrustfully.

"How many other Dorians can there be? This isn't Eastenders." I say, pulling out my own phone to text this two-timing, flip-flopping, tea-and-crumpets-eating motherfucker.

"Dorian Gray? With an A?" Asher asks, now in front of me.

"Oh, Praise Jeebus. No, mine's with an E. He's very proper. Very posh. Pinkies up, all that." I say, a wave of relief washing over me.

"That son of a-, JJ, it's the same lying, cheating asshole," Asher says, her grip tightening on her drink.

I know that grip. I watch Basketball Wives. I'm not for play-play. So I decided to let my tongue throw the first punch.

"Nah nah nah. There's no way in hell. No one would ever cheat on me. All my prospective gentlemen callers are warned way ahead of time that I will burn their family's houses down and dig up their grandparents just out of principle."

I take a deep inhale.

"Besides, what would he want with *you* when he has *this?*"

Asher slams her drink on the bar, marches up and glares at me from her freakishly low vantage point.

"Maybe he wanted some ASS with his crazy! Not to mention these titties!" Asher yelled, mock-fondling her breasts like she was bringing watermelons to the Jukebox Jamboree.

A crowd of slack-jawed gawkers was starting to gather around the commotion, coaxing us on.

"How dare he play me? I'm unplayable. Not for play-play, level 9000." I declare.

She grabbed her phone again and started to jab her tiny little doll hands at her screen.

"And this mother fucker doesn't want to pick up his phone!" She yelled out, frustratedly, her eyes going glassy.

She let out a low, little emotional sob– but not like a feminine one, one that kinda sounded like a baby bear calling for its mother.

"What do you have that I don't?" she asked, as tears began to form in her eyes.

"A dick, Asher. A dick." I say, pragmatically.

Asher stifles her sobs and makes the *welp* face before she reaches for her drink again.

"And what a dick!" yelled out some shaved ape in leather pants from the other side of the bar.

"You wish, Roger!" I yell out before I turn back to Asher and say, "So now what?"

She finishes typing something on her phone before she smugly tucks her phone back in her cleavage and knocks back the rest of her drink. Venom drips off of her as she leaves the bar and yells back,

"I have to pee!" to no one in particular.

I heavily sigh and prepare myself for what I know is already there. I open Facebook, and the first thing that pops up is a post from Asher from one minute ago. In that span of four seconds, she had already composed a scathing, not-so-subliminal post directed at yours truly.

Asher Dark:

Be careful who you call bestie, cuz one day that bestie may become a worstie and SLEEP WITH YOUR VERY BRITISH MAN. Also, he makes way too many pansexual jokes, but gets away with it because he says it's cute when he does it. Newsflash: @phrique it isn't always cute when you do it. And by the way, I smoked with that lovely drag queen, and they're right, you do have a lesbian haircut! YOU BITCH!

I inhaled the stink of beer burps and someone's horrible walk-by-air until my chest ached.

"YOU TAGGED ME?!"

I waited for the stars to dissipate so I could chase her ass down. I marched up to the ladies' bathroom and pounded on the door.

"ASHER! TAKE THAT SHIT DOWN RIGHT NOW! BEFORE MY PR REP SEES IT!"

"Fuck you JJ!"

She yelled back through the door. I pushed, finding it locked, vexing me further. I could hear her crying through the door. *The stupid Pisces in me instantly felt bad, but also really wanted to kick this door down for that lesbian haircut line. No one ever talks about the difficulty of being an intuitive and empathic Pisces, who also wants to snap anyone's neck that even looks at them funny.*

I started to kinda feel sorry for myself for a split second when I heard a definite poot from behind the door.

"BITCH! IS YOU SHITTING IN THE CLUB?! WHERE THEY DO THAT AT?! IN THE MIDDLE OF OUR FIGHT SCENE?!"

She sniffled and let another one go before she replied,

"This is too much for one person to handle, and bitch, you know I have a nervous stomach."

I hear a commotion coming from the bar, but I'm trying to keep Asher from spiraling out. She was my ride home after all.

"I know you," she grunted, "found out I was dating Dorian somehow!" She sniffled, "I would expect this from that droopy-faced bitch or that other catty bitch, but not you! I trusted you! I was going to ask if you wanted to collab on a book with me!"

My face was a portrait of perplexity after hearing all this. How could she think that I did this on purpose? There's nothing I hated more than when someone had a misapprehension about me. I didn't know Dorian was seeing anyone else, but I had my suspicions. *I just wanted a British boyfriend so I could catch him not doing the accent. Then I'd have proof & they can stop lying to all of us. The sex was just an added bonus.*

There was a crowd forming behind me, all mumbling to themselves. The shitty trance music had stopped. *Hopefully, the DJ died or something.* Ugh, I had to fix this. I thought long and hard about what to say.

"Asher!" I yelled through the door, waiting for her response.

I heard her little boohoo wolverine whimper so I figured she was still emotional.

"How soon do you want to do that collab, cause I am positively bedeviled with deadlines. Maybe we can do it after I finish one of my other nine current WIPs?" I said, in my best consolatory tone. "Nothing about women trapped in basements, please! That's tired. That's played. We deserve better!"

Just as I was about to suggest a cursed TV script idea, I felt angry blue-collar mitts grab me from behind. Before I even had time to turn and yell for them to buy me a drink first, I was being roughly guided toward the back of the club. I heard Asher finally respond in an angry, "Biiiiiiiitch" but I was too stunned to respond. It all happened so fast, I barely had time to see the brute who was manhandling me and pushing me through the crowd of people. The glow of the exit sign illuminated my angry expression when I finally got my bearings and turned toward the Neanderthal bouncer.

It was too late; the meathead had already given me the final shove that sent me flying out of the service door entrance and into the cold, nasty alley. In the commotion, I tripped over my big ass shoes and skidded on the gravelly concrete, right into a puddle. I welcomed death before I even landed.

The cock-eyed cretin pulled the gnarled cigar from where his side teeth once were and yelled, "And stay out!" before slamming the door shut.

I turned away and winced from shame, not for my actions, but for how corny that shit was. I stood up and dusted myself off, vowing to get back in the club and light this Looney Tune wiseguy's ass *UP* when I see him again. My hip bone ached as I tried to brush the pebbly dirt off my filthy shorts. I landed on that shit with all my weight and would definitely be feeling that in the morning.

I pounded on the door a few times, knowing no one would open it. I tried a few more times before my dainty fist ached. I stopped and rubbed it, looking around for some other possible entrance. There had to be some way, because I was *not* about to walk through this dark ass alley. I turned to look down the other direction, leading to the street, when I caught some kind of motion in the inky darkness. My heart began to race, and I quickly got back to pounding on the door. I heard gravel-scraping steps coming closer, but I dared not look, out of fear that I would inevitably stare *the killer* in the face.

My mind was on cruise control as I thrashed and threw myself against the door. The sound of my creeping death in the form of shuffling, heavy footsteps was only drowned out by my screams for help, and that I was too young to die. My incessant, manic pounding only ceased when the figure from the darkness finally stepped into the light, stifling me.

"Hey, man, keep it down. They're never gonna let you in dressed like that," came from a wet-sounding froggish voice that bristled jerkily in my ears.

I slowly turned, preparing my nerves to meet my alley amigo. My blood ran cold as I saw the shaggy man sauntering closer to me in his tattered rags.

"A HOBO!" I yell out, fighting the urge to clamp my filthy hands against my cheeks in dramatic horror or pass out as my body slumps against the rusty door.

Instead, I dramatically hold the back of my hands to my head to stop myself from fainting.

"We prefer to be called unhoused now," he said curtly.

I relent a little, my rationale cutting through my absurd, made-up fear of homeless people.

"I just said-"

"UNHOUSED, SORRY!" I shout, still pressed against the door.

I can hear noise coming from inside, but the thick security door won't let me identify it. My eyes dart in every direction; not wanting to stare at the poor, *FUCK, I mean, the destitute man.*

"You're not scared of ol' Jerry, are you?" he asked in an odd, slightly slurred sing-song way.

"No, I used to be. Well, no. I thought I was. I just...When I was little, I wanted to help the homeless, but then I found out that I can't help everyone. In my all-or-nothing little mind, I just said it would be better to avoid thinking about it. So when I saw a homeless person, I would lock up because I didn't know how to deal with it all. Fucking Pisces shit, I-"

During my rambling, *ol' Jerry* had gotten closer to me. He was now directly in front of me, close enough to see the crazed look in his eyes and his ticking, toothless smile that made my skin crawl. I internally screamed through a beat of silence, but he just stood there with his head cocked and stared me down. My nerves made me word-vomit more.

"I even wrote a story called Hobophobia. It was very gross and bloody, my first splatterpunk story ever. It was very cathartic for me, actually." I said, while I pounded my heel on the door.

"Is that so?" Jerry said, taking another step closer to me. "Did you publish it yet? Huh? Did you publish Hobophobia yet? The very cathartic, bloody, gory, patronizing, but as long as it makes *you* feel better about that classist, judgemental, grandiose brain of yours?"

I gasped and choked out, "No...not yet, but...my friend Zaq read it and..."

"Not yet doesn't coooooouunnt." Jerry bellowed with his best Brandy impression. His stench permeated my space more than his imposing position just inches from me.

My mind was reeling as my skin started to tingle and my vision went staticky again. Just like before, in the...bathroom.

"Nononononoooo!" I groan, using the last of my strength to pummel the door once more until my fists start to bleed. That's when Jerry began to cough, hack, and take a step closer. His feet were practically touching mine. He covered his mouth, poorly – *OH GOD!* – with his grimy hand. I tried to dodge his germs, flipping my head back and forth as I could feel our shared breathing air being contaminated with pestilence beyond my comprehension. I heard a commotion from behind the door, which gave me a sliver of hope. It sounded like someone was yelling inside.

My body flooded with joy as I heard the door rattle and begin to push out. The thumping music and laughing screams poured into the dank space. Then the motion caught me and I realized that I would be pushed onto Jerry and-

I let out a garbled, manly shriek as I was throttled into the arms of my unhoused homie, fighting my damndest to find my equilibrium. In the unexpected shift, he caught me and stared into my eyes. *He caught me. He saved me. Was I? Was this? Was I about to make out with a total stranger at a club? Welp, no different than what most of these hoes did*, I justified.

Jerry stood me upright and dusted me off, jolting me out of my weird romantic stupor, and stared at my mouth. I mean, it is pretty; I don't blame him, but-

"You got a hair on your lip," Jerry said, still a bit slurred.

Then he brought his crusty thumb up to my face and gingerly wiped it across my lip, to my stunned horror.

"Beggar."

He whispered, like the old man in the movie *Thinner*, as I felt the remnants of my nightmares coat my perfectly balmed, quivering lip. My body went rigid, the air left my body, and my legs gave out from under me. As I felt myself falling back, my eyes fixated on Jerry's slumped face. The side of his head seemed to be melting down and joining his neck, almost like he was collapsing in on himself.

I felt my body bumping into others and someone screaming, "Oh God! Close the door! Don't let the homeless guy in!"

"Unhoused!" Jerry and I screamed.

A set of hands caught me before I hit the ground, but all I could see was the slightest hint of Jerry's smile under his dissolving facade, going dark as the door slammed shut again.

The low lights of the rear hallway made it hard to focus, and the thumping music made my head throb. I felt so discombobulated, the room was spinning.

Whoever caught me pulled me to my feet. I stood there a second, trying to figure out what the fuck just happened. My skin felt hot, yet clammy at the same time. My wide eyes flashed to the door as I used my shirt to wipe whatever leftover foot, mouth, and ass disease Jerry spread across my lip. I paused when I caught a glimpse of my shadowed reflection in the dirty mirrored walls. I took a few befuddled steps toward it, watching my swollen lip swelling up in real time. Panic rocked my system as my throat started to burn. Suddenly, my chest felt like it seized, and I couldn't stop coughing. I leaned down, trying to collect myself. At least trying to get the coughing to stop.

"OMG, cover your fucking mouth," some trout yelled uncouthly.

I think I just contracted the hobo plague hoe. Shut the fuck up talking to me.

The hulking mass that was the punk ass Looney-Tunes-wiseguy-ass-bouncer walked up behind me and put his overgrown dick-beater on my shoulder.

"Boss said to bring you up fron-" was all he got out before I pulled back and lobbed my fist at his bulbous Adam's apple.

I landed a direct hit, watching his lummox ass double over and cough as much as I just did. I watched in stunned horror as a greenish pallor washed over my fist and arm from the flash of a strobe light. Panic began to sink in when another coughing fit hit me, and I doubled over. By the time my lungs finished recovering, I looked at my palms again and turned to look at my reflection. My lip was back to normal, and so was my skin. Whatever hobo bug I caught seemed to have passed through in record time. Praise be to my go-go-gadget immune system and chia seeds!

I applied a schmear of lip chap to my recovered lips and gave myself a once-over. Ready to make my exit before that cretinous bouncer bounced his Neanderthal ass back up. That's when the lull of a song transition allowed me to hear the coughing fits of the other shadowy figures in this cramped hall. My eyes metronomed back and forth as

I turned, trying to configure the best escape route through the writhing masses blocking my way back to the main club space. The strobing lights weren't doing me any favors.

"Clear a path, trollops! Let's get all these SHEIN boots out of the way!" I yelled bluntly.

The thrashing bodies kept gyrating and obstructing my escape as the music volume and my panic heightened.

"Y'all blocking a fire exit, you know, Jesus be a fire extinguisher if any of these synthetic fibers gets near an open flame!"

I continue to shout to no avail, pushing past the sickly, clammy, intertwined limbs. A wet cough echoes a few inches from my ear, making my *fight or fight* instinct kick in. At this point, I feel like I'm climbing over meaty, crunching chunks of quicksand. I'm throwing as many sharp elbows as I can, just trying to see the light at the end of this claustrophobic tunnel of uncouth and unmoving livestock.

"And cover your motherfucking mouths! You hoes know we are still in a pandemic, right?!"

Just as I begin to make progress, a damp catcher's mitt of flesh clamps down on me. *A-fucking-gain?* My crazed mind thinks, as I smell the familiar body spray of the manhandling bouncer with boundary issues, mixed with a foreign, sharp odor that was infiltrating my nostrils. For the first time, in a long time—or like four minutes ago—

I turned slowly, unsure of what my eyes were about to behold. The sucking sounds and a resonating wheeze did *not* bode well.

Staring back at me were the glowing white eyes of the bouncer who couldn't take a hint, which only flickered for a moment as his nose and cheeks cascaded down his face in a growing lesion before the sheet of flesh sloughed off his blindingly white skull. A wave of vertigo hit me as I pulled back, feeling sickly green bits of his hand and fingers come with me. My shoulders pulled up next to my ears as my face puckered into a sphincter of revulsion and fear. The wall of bodies around me locked in place, unable to escape as I watched the jolly green giant let out a final hack, spraying me with putrescent puke before he unceremoniously keeled over on top of me.

The momentum of his towering topple cleared a small path behind me, sending the throngs of bodies out of our way. While I did my best to recover, with mucosal film filled with dislodged teeth and bits of congealed organs strewn about, I trudged closer to my way out. The lights above began to shine in full power, flooding the space with light, to my exhausted dismay. Birthed from the bowels of hell itself, what had incubated in the darkness came to unsettling fruition in the light.

Whatever Unhoused Jerry had passed through me was not having the same effect on the other club-goers. Jerking bodies motioned toward me. Bodies contorted in shuddering stages of decay all began to gravitate my way, the only able-bodied would-be-survivor. My mind felt ready to snap, crawling over crackling and popping bodies, putrid cuddle puddles straight out of my nightmares. Hyperventilating, but doing my best to hold all of my body fluids within me. I was determined to escape this labyrinth of leprous lichens.

Arduously traversing the mounds of disintegrating bodies below me, I finally saw the gaudy glowing lasers that promised me reprieve. I continued to army crawl through the sludge of 20-something's, wriggling flesh, and countless costume jewelry pieces, before I made it to the edge and rolled out onto the filthy floor. With my last shred of energy, I stood up and ran through the somehow uninfected crowd to the bar.

"Tequila and ice!" I yell at the startled bartender, raking bits of gore out of my bang with my quivering fingers.

"Pineapple juice and grenadine, if you have it," I add, still trying to catch my breath.

Snatching it out of his hand before he can even set it down on the lacquered bar top.

"Is...that..." the bartender said, pointing at my bloody hand, chugging my drink before I responded to him.

"Yeah, it's a pineapple tequila sunrise, I call it a Tequila Sunbeam." I say before I choke down the last of it and turn away from the still staring bartender.

"Now where the fuck did Asher go?!" I yell out to no one in particular.

10

Unbreak My Heart, Zombie Nana

Asher

My stomach hurts like a sum-bitch. Not only is my poor butthole Hershey squirting, but I'm squatting over the toilet, praying to whatever poop gods there are that I don't spray the back of the fucking wall and turn it into some kind of abstract kid's paint project. My bowels have betrayed me, yet again. Possibly from that weird ass shot or because of my nerves. My other bodily fluids have betrayed me as well. My eyes are puffy from the tears that spill down, smearing my eyeliner. Thank Papa Satan for waterproof mascara or else I would end up looking like Art the Clown and terrify my bestie. Well, ex-bestie.

I hate this shit. It feels like an asteroid blasted through the atmosphere and crashed into my heart, completely obliterating it, like the dinosaurs.

Yeah, I should probably take my post down, but damnit! He knows the Gemini inside me fights battles, and occasionally the not-so-good twin wins.

I angrily text Dorian again. I know he received my messages, but the mother fucking Lord Cunt Nuggets probably left me on read. Didn't he see that documentary about that chick who went crazy over being left on read?

It feels like someone has ripped open my ribcage and yanked my heart right out. There was a time my heart was so full of love and now it's just a dark cave containing the echoes of my loneliness.

I was falling in love with Dorian. It was something beautiful and unexpected. He wasn't the typical type of guy I would go for. I could be myself with him. I told him everything about my past—all the dark things about my childhood and my years as a homeless teenager.

I vented to him about my mentors; the one who turned out to be a fucking predator and the other one, making me feel like I was special, then turned on me and lied about me. Just because he didn't have the balls to tell the truth and instead tried to make me out to be a pervert. Just once, I would love for these men to get what's coming to them, but that never seems to be the case. They always wiggle out of it one way or another.

Not this fucking time though. Dicks are getting smashed tonight. My horrible fucking track record with predators was over.

Maybe JJ was right, and I really am a lesbian. I should be, goddamnit. I could write a whole ass book just on the fucked up things I've gone through in my life.

I never wanted to care for Dorian, and I damn sure wasn't thinking about dating when we met. All I cared about was writing *Lucifur*. I should have known better when those gorgeous eyes locked on me. He broke every wall I had carefully stacked over the last something-something years.

Devastated was an understatement. Not to mention the double-edged sword, and my supposed best friend. I hate my beautifully-haired, two-faced bestie. *Not really, but damn.* I want to bite his smug face off. How could he do this to me? After all I've been through with friendships and the hard work I've done for over a fucking year on myself. He was there for me, cheering me on when I didn't even cheer for myself.

He has the nerve to try and be funny. Bitch, I know I'm taking forever on this new collab but...I don't know. My brain hasn't been working right and I'm just now getting back to myself. I used to be able to bang out books like it wasn't shit, but I've barely put anything out. I lost my mojo for a bit, being stuck in a deep depression and feeling outcasted and rejected. That thought really makes me think of mine and JJ's friendship. *Like really think about it.*

This doesn't make sense. If he knew, why would he even agree to meet with me? He hates drama. I just don't see him doing that to me. He's far from dumb. He may be this bougie diva with a sharp tongue, but he isn't a bad person. *I know that in my heart.*

Yes, obviously, over-trusting has led me astray before, but something inside me is arguing ferociously that he didn't know. I've never been the friend that people couldn't live without. I was their friend until they found something better. I never really fit in, I was the best friend out of convenience. I have a few people outside of the author world, but not ones that check on me every day. Hell, every week or month at that. JJ makes me feel as if I dropped off the face of the earth, it would matter to him.

This shit has my blood pressure up and my mind all over the place. I take the damn post down before he has time to find a scathing GIF to reply with.

I wipe, flush with my boot, and sling the stall open. I'm thankful that the bathrooms are silver and black instead of gold. Sleek and shiny, with a hint of darkness. The stalls are shiny silver with black sinks and floor. The walls are white, but with more paintings of fancy fuckers all dolled up. I approach the four black sinks that line the wall and avoid the single giant mirror above them.

I lather my hands with some sweet-smelling soap and sigh before I look at myself in the mirror. I fully expect to see my reflection staring back at me. A tear-stained, black streaked face, but that's not the image I find. I feel locked in terror.

When I was five, I started to have this nightmare. My grandma was a big part of my life. We are country yeet-haw motherfuckers, so it's either Memaw or Nana. For me, it was Nana. She and my Papa got me every weekend. I loved them so much. They treated me like their beautiful little princess. Life was perfect until I started to have the dream.

It starts with me waking up and getting out of my Sesame Street bedsheets. I tiptoe in my CareBears nightgown over to my bedroom window. When I go to bed, it's night of course, but in my dream, it's always daytime. Instead of the normal view of a yard and playground,–I see a vast, sweltering desert. The rays of the sun are blistering. I can feel them on my tiny face through the glass. There is a white shed to the right and nothing else but swirling dancing sand.

It all comes rushing back to me at this moment because that's exactly what I'm seeing in front of me, but that's impossible. I'm staring into the mirror in the bathroom of the Clurb and I know I'm awake. I start to shake, my pulse racing. I want to run away, but just like in the dream, I am rooted to the ground. Invincible, powerful hands holding me in place.

Just like my bedroom window, the view of the mirror changes, but it's subtle. You know when something is different but off? You can't quite figure it out until you see a figure come into view. At first, it's tiny, but then I recognize it as it comes closer. I've had this dream for over thirty years now. I've just come to terms with it; it'll never go away. My whole life, it has haunted me. Even more so, now that Nana is gone.

By now, the figure, my Nana, has made it halfway through the desert. The first time I had this dream, it took me a moment to realize something was wrong with her. Instead of her full, smiling cheeks, her face is sunken in and parts of the left side of her head are missing. Blackness oozes from where her skin should be, and her perfectly permed hair is molting away in patches. Her eyes are the scariest part - there was nothing there. Her lovely brown eyes that had stared at me with so much love and pride are gone. What's left are twin pools of a dismal, blackened abyss whose whispers chill my bones. The absent honey-hued glint of joy that echoed the smile she once held in those eyes for the granddaughter, whom she raised. The only emotion that registers from within the chasms is pure malice. Her perfect leather jacket, which she wore with pride, is in tatters, swaying with the breeze. Her ripped white jeans show blood-stained bone showing through the left one, and one of her white Keds is missing. Her skeletal foot is turned at an unnatural angle as she trudges closer, with a small, crispy hop in her step.

The sand swirls around her few staggered steps until she disappears in the incoming sandstorm. My eyes can't stop scanning this landscape until I catch sight of her again. The extreme winds seem to have taken her with it. In a blast of gritty wind, she appears dangerously closer now.

I'm that terrified little girl again. My heartbeat turns into Lightning McQueen. I feel it beating so fast, it feels like it's about to burst from my chest and do a burnout trying to get away. *Skurrt skurrt!*

The hair on my arms do not just raise, they tingle. They vibrate. The bathroom door bursts open. Three ladies, along with the loud noise from the clurb enter. I must have looked crazy, staring into the mirror with my mouth gaping and shaking like a wet cat. A tall blonde in stilettos and a short silver miniskirt that looks like something more for an alien convention than a fancy pants club speaks to me.

"Are you ok, ma'am?"

Bless her heart.

I'm about to say something when the brunette to her left lets out a gasp and points to the mirror.

All at once, the other women turn to look. *Me too, bitch. I wanna see.*

A giant wave ripples through the framed desert, creating a sand tsunami that slams against the mirror like a window, filling the view with nothing but sand until the entire thing goes black. We all trade glances, silently asking if we'd all just seen that with our eyes. A crack rings out and echoes like a gunshot.

Not this shit again!

The darkened glass spider webs and shatters under the pressure. An explosion of broken glass and sizzling desert sand spills out, blasting us all, knocking two of the girls into each other. Their skulls collide, eliciting a hampered knock as they topple to the floor, and the room begins to fill with sand.

The blonde and the last brunette stand and try to plod their way toward the door. Blondie is struggling ahead of her friend until the girl yanks her ponytail and pulls her back. The last brunette gains enough leverage to pull herself out of the sand successfully.

I watch in horror as the sand swelling below them slurps them down, becoming quicksand before my eyes. The last brunette pulls her screaming friend down with her. Ponytail still in hand, as the sweltering sand fills their screaming mouths.

I struggle to pull myself out of the dune as the sand stops spilling out of the empty hollow on the wall. It feels like it takes a lifetime, but eventually I'm shakily standing on a small mound. Relief washes over me momentarily until I feel a hand gently resting on my shoulders. I warily look over to see skeletal fingers, and begin to scream my lungs out.

Something you should know about me–if JJ hadn't made it abundantly clear–I have a raspy voice. I can't scream at all. My sister used to make fun of me growing up. She said I sounded like a dog with its bark clipped or whatever you call it. I don't like that shit. Who does that? The dogs got to bark. It's what fucking dogs do.

Anyway, back to my crisis.

I swear my soul leaves my body and travels around the world seventy-two times before returning. I lunge forward, dashing away from that wretched hand.

"Don't turn away from me! I raised you! You, Rob, and Sierra. Your whore of a mother wasn't around was she?"

My nana ended up raising me and my siblings, along with our daddy. She hated my Mama for a long time for leaving us. It's one of the reasons I have abandonment issues, or so I have been told by a therapist. Anyway, they would get into literal fist fights back then, scrapping like chickens. Eventually Nana got diagnosed with dementia. My siblings and I took turns taking care of her until she passed. There are things I experienced during that time that will haunt me for the rest of my life. Her last months on this earth were rough, not just for her, but for all of us.

Seeing this vision come to life– knowing that she is really gone now–it's almost my undoing. I want to curl up in a fetal position and bawl my eyes out. My knees get weak, and my heart is heavy. My heartbeat stutters, my whole body, reverberating at my core. *This has been too much today. What the fuck is going on? This can't be fucking real.* Lost in thought, I feel a sharp pain and look down.

Goddamn Zombie Nana is munching on my arm like it's a juicy, buttery corncob. I ball up my fist and hit her in the side of the face, but instead of her head bouncing to the side–like I'd imagined–my fist goes right through her cheek. Mortified, I pull my fist back and stare at the maroon goo coating my hand. A chunk of decayed tooth slides down my pinky. I damn near puked.

I try to back away but trip on something sticking out of the sand, landing on my ass. My hand gets coated in sand like a piece of chicken ready for the fryer. I wiped it on my skirt and looked back to see what tripped me.

A pale hand with hot pink, manicured nails, attached to a slender arm sporting a VIP bracelet on the wrist, is wriggling out of the sand. I crawl forward, straining, pulling, trying to free this poor girl from her sandy tomb as Night of the Living Nana shuffles towards us. Another hand breaks through the sand. I grab onto both of them, pulling with everything I have until her head surfaces.

As soon as it pops out of the sand and I see her face I let go. She snaps her head forward, gnashing her teeth at me. *This bitch is a goddamn zombie too?!* Her scalp is peeled back halfway but I notice the blonde ponytail bobbing behind her. Blood mixed with sand coats the front part of her head, where the skin and hair parted.

Damn that bitch who pulled her in had almost snatched her shit off!

I jump to my feet *(we are going to pretend my knees actually work)*, lifting my right boot before I kick at her face so hard that her head topples off and rolls right between Dawn of The Nana's feet.

The ghoul masquerading as Nana picks up the head, applies pressure to both sides, and effortlessly cracks it open like a pecan. She angrily digs her hand into one side of the broken skull and scoops up a handful of brains before she shovels them in her gaping maw. As she chews, some of it falls out of the hole in her face I created when I struck her. More gloops down her jaw and collarbone. I am frozen. I want to run to the door, but my stupid little stubby legs won't move. Nana drops the splintered halves after licking them clean before running straight at me like an enraged bull.

Stupid, frozen me doesn't budge. She tackles me and we both fall to the floor. She lies on top of me, jaws and teeth snapping at me like fucking Cujo. Some of the unswallowed brain slops out of her mouth and slaps onto my forehead. In my mind, an alarm goes off. Everything goes red, and I fight like I've never fought before. Like mother fucking Mike Tyson, I open wide and I bite her ass. You wanna eat me? Nah bitch *(sorry Nana)*, I'm going to eat yo ass.

I tear into her neck with my teeth, while wrapping my arms around her, rolling both of our bodies until I am on top of her. I'm glaring down at what was once the woman who loved me, and sang me *Lonely Little Robin* when I was sick. I raise both my fists and bring them down on the woman who would have fist-fought the whole world for me. I repeat my slams on her pulverized face as a guttural, anguished scream rolls up my throat and bursts through my lips. I keep hitting and wailing on her until her face is nothing but mush. My fists are busted with bleeding knuckles. Tears pour from my eyes. Rivers of pain and loss spill down my cheeks and onto what remains of the woman who gave up everything to be my everything.

Sitting back on my legs, I close my eyes. Put my face in my ruined hands and sob.

My torment is shattered by a scream. I open my eyes, and Zombie Nana is gone. The sand has disappeared, and the mirror is intact. My bleeding, Nana-covered knuckles are back to normal.

In the corner are the girls who were swallowed up by the sand. The very much alive zombie girl is on the floor with her knees pulled up to her chest, screaming and crying while her two friends stand over her, trying to help her.

"My hair! Get away from me." She screams, pushing her away, scratching at her VIP wrist band.

I am either losing my goddamn mind or something fucked up is going on in this clurb. I need to find JJ and figure out what the fuck is going on. I reach into my Tiddy and pull out a blunt.

First things first.

I need to get my mind right and calm my beating heart before I have a stroke. It's time to get high.

I open the bathroom door and run into a wall. Not really a wall, just two club hoes trying to get into the bathroom. One is the girl from earlier who looks like my wifey, *Mariah Carey.* She's dressed in a black lace catsuit, and the other has a bright orange bob cut wig that matches her stripper heels. The neon hot pink halter dress cradles her curves spectacularly.

I swear, when the one in the lace looked at me, her eyes glowed bright red for a second, but I knew I had already been seeing shit. So I figured this was just something else to add to the list of freaky what-the-fuck things for tonight's escapade.

"My bad, ladies," I mumble as I scoot past them and go smoke my blunt.

I'm probably going to need another cigarette too. I scratch my wrist and notice a rash has started forming where the VIP bracelet rubbed.

"I gotta get this mother fucker off," I grumble to myself as I go outside.

11

This Tangled Web is Unbeweavable

PHRIQUE

Dorian, idk what makes you think avoiding me is going to save your elderly ho ass, but if you don't show your bitch ass face I will burn this OSHA nightmare to the ground. & I'll get away with it too, mark my words.

Except for this damning text, fuck. I should have eaten before I drank. Now I'm bitter AND belligerent. More than usual.

Also, fuck you for making me break my no white boy rules. The pink ones always weirded me out anyways.

I flashed my VIP bracelet to the hot-dog-necked lunk standing guard behind the velvet rope, who reluctantly let me through. Giving him my meanest *"you don't want none of this smoke trust and believe booboo"* three-second stare. Don't let the immaculate bone structure fool you, I will...pay someone to fuck you up...I have pretty knuckle tattoos and I'm not fucking them up for some one-syllable toting, neanderthal lackey.

I made it upstairs to the extremely bougie glass enclosure that seemed like it was made for me. Like the perfect villain headquarters, made to watch and talk shit from afar. The couches were a bit kitsch. As were the old portraits of dusty-looking white people, some shrouded and some not. Interesting *choices* indeed. As I made it around the other VIPs, looking for Asher, I decided to cut through the middle. A large golden griffin statue stood gauchely in the center of the room, staring me down with its penetrating gaze. I flicked my perfectly painted middle finger against it; gold-plated as well. *Bless their hearts.* Probably for the best, because any heavier and this little glass terrarium was going to be the scene of a bloody, bougie massacre.

I made it around the statue after a herd of grazing heifers finally got the clue to—mayhaps—not stand in the middle of a room. *Spatial awareness and common decency are a thing, after all.* After a full revolution around the gaudy space, *Still no Asher. Where the hell was this hoe?*

I started to feel woozy and pulled out my phone, figuring she had to have texted me. Maybe she left? Maybe I went a bit too far with my delightful dry humor? She was visibly hurt, as was I, but she didn't do anything wrong here. That no good Yorkshire terrier of a man was to blame here, not us.

My eyes wouldn't focus on my screen again, and I made the executive decision that I was indeed tipsy in the clurb, at my big age. *My, how the mighty have fallen.* I turned towards the VIP bar to grab a water. Seeing the spicy lil' bartender lighting a row of drinks, letting a barrage of flame poofs light up the already cramped space. More people had entered VIP since I first ventured up here, and like clockwork, I looked down at the glass floor and swore I heard little crackles as the vertigo hit me.

That's it. I'm outty. I've seen this movie multiple times. Not my gay ass.

I made it to the exit, passing through before I yelled out,

"Enjoy your death trap, ladies!"

Precariously making my way back downstairs, through the barrage of lasers and thumping bass. I heard a few trouts from above fire back at my fashionable exit.

"What was her problem?"

"Lesbian haircut? Who wears shorts to a nightclub?"

I grit my teeth and seethe. They were lucky I was dazed and on a mission to find my friend, or I would have let them all have it. *No matriarchs of their families would be spared.* I make it to the ground floor, and the lunk with the asymmetrical blink lets me pass.

This game of chasing the diminutive person of short stature, who may or may not lead me to a pot of gold or possibly her lucky charms, is eventually testing even my suspension of disbelief. What is this, like five chapters of slapstick serendipitous "missed her by this much" schtick? Oh, wait, that's right; I was feeling hella disoriented.

Everything seemed hazy, I was confused, and I was drifting in and out of delusions of horrific grandeur. *More than usual.* Had I been drugged? Did I somehow end up in a made-for-TV Lifetime Movie? *The Wrong Clurb? Not Without My Disco balls?* I took the last swallow of my Tequila Sunbeam, then I stared at it hard. *All I had to drink was this and...*

My wristband began to itch like crazy again. My sweat and whatever leftover alley grime on my wrist made it swell up something awful. I did what I could to pull it off–I ain't going back up to that hot breath observatory again–but it wouldn't budge. I grit my teeth and notice a door to the side of the club that's lit up with outdoor lights.

Of course! Her ass has to be out there smoking, or **smoking**, *as always. Why didn't I think of that in the first place? Plus, I'm sure she had a pair of scissors or a switchblade in them tiddies, cuz heaven forbid she bring a handbag.*

I make it outside, relieved that the cool night air makes me feel a little better. There's a decent crowd, but no

Asher that I can see among the whirling spotlights. *Fuck, I need a place to sit down.* Making my way through the crowd to the side of the building, where I see little trees and a few puffs of smoke coming from some benches.

Ugh, what are we...our age? Who sits in a clurb?

I see my little goth nugget of joy, smoking away and tapping on her phone.

"Bitch!" I yell, which makes half of the patio area pause and look our way.

"Biiiiiitch," rumbles from her otherworldly, raspy vocal cords, which made the nosey-ass patio gawkers turn back around.

I can see tears in her eyes, which is never good, so I prepare myself...time to be human again, or at least pretend to be.

"I was looking all over for you, dammit, you won't believe the shit that has happened tonight," I say as I dust off the seat next to her...*idk who all been out here or how they live.*

She chuckles gruffly and sputters, "Bitch, you ain't the only one."

She takes a deep inhale off her burnt celery scented devil's lettuce spliff.

"This night went to shit. All I was trying to do was make up with your ass, so we could get back to normal."

I nod, trying to wipe a stain off my already ruined shoes.

"Whose bright idea was it to come to this trifling ass club? At our big ages? We been knew. If you pee when you sneeze and you like soup a little too much, you need to keep your geriatric asses at home." I say as we shakily stand with a cacophony of knee pops.

There's an uncomfortable silence and a cough from the crowd behind us. Asher giggles.

"Well, there's still time, let's fucking go."

"I'm glad you said it first, cuz chiiiild." I say, yawning and stretching.

"Hell yeah. We grown, fuck this club and its bastard of an owner."

The pain hit us both in the gut. I think we both forgot that part.

A random girl with a very avian nose swoops in and takes a picture of us, blinding us with the flash off an old Polaroid camera. We both blink away the stars, as well as the confusion. Where could anyone find such an ancient relic? We groggily watch her fanning the developing picture in her hand.

"It'll be on the picture wall inside, mmk?" She screeched before she sped off inside.

"Bruh. I'm still just... I don't know how this shit happened, but I think we should go find that flip-flopping fancy fuck and teach his ass a lesson. You know I hate being petty, but..."

Asher stubbed her blunt out and flicked it in the plant next to her.

"Let's get our asses back inside before lightning strikes your petty ass, please. Then we are gonna fuck him up, go find us some food, and take our asses home. Deal?"

"Deal," I say as I help my best decrepit, elderly friend back inside Club Hedonia.

"Oh yeah, do you have something I can cut this bracelet off with? It's making my shit itchy as hell."

"Yeah, I got you boo," Asher says, digging half of her arm in her cleavage and pulling out a box cutter.

I hold my wrist out to her, "I'll let you—uh—do the honors."

She places the blunt side of the blade under the glowing bracelet on my wrist and pulls it up and away as it falls to the ground.

"I took mine off too; that shit was giving me hives."

We made it to the doors of the patio when a series of crashes resounded from inside and the ground below us shook. Asher had her hand on the door, but she looked at me nervously. I nod at her to open it.

"What more could this hellacious night bring?" I say, ignorantly.

The horrible music hadn't stopped, but we could see a few clusters of panicked club-goers. Asher stops to check on a group of girls she met in the ladies' room, one of the fourteen times she was in there. I sneak off to see how our picture came out. Praying my hair looks good in it at least. I find the pic pinned to the very top of a series of polaroids taken throughout the night. Both of our eyes are closed, and I look like shit, microwaved. I balked to no one in particular, heading back to tell Asher that we need to do a retake before we go.

I'm about to cross the dance floor to rejoin Asher when a group of dude-bros near the tables begins shouting. They're trying to calm one of their own down, as I try to skirt past because I don't wanna get anything else on me. This guy—in his little brother's t-shirt—is standing on the booth seat, looking around the room with paranoia-stricken eyes.

"How do you not see them?!" He yells out, climbing to the upper part of the booth, not taking his eyes off some invisible entity.

"It's a fucking cockroach as big as a Rottweiler!"

I give the invisible camera my patented *Hell-ToTheNawToTheNawNawNaw* side eye and almost make it past them when something skitters across the floor. In response, the screaming Chad grabs the oversized golden scimitar hanging on the wall and slices toward the tabletop.

"Asher!" I yell out in the rising panic. "These white folks is crazy!"

I lost sight of her, looking back just long enough to see this crazed man swing the razor-sharp sword again with all his might. The sound of yelling and squelching can be heard as his three frat bros look down at their white polos, quickly turning red. All three of them gawk down at their torsos when their shirts and skins open, letting their intestines slop out onto the floor beneath them. I got sprayed, mainly in the face by the three frat bros. Like I was on some bad pornhub stream and I really needed the cash. Thankfully, I closed my mouth for once.

Before the new trauma and blood stains have time to set in, I try to get as far away from the boy band turned crimson sprinklers.

An ear-aching buzzing sound pours through the space, making everyone in earshot wince in pain. I made it between the bar and the exit when—to my horror—the discoball displays around the club began to shake and crackle.

"Fuck fuck fuck fuck, ASHER!" I yell, running for the door before the nearest disco ball erupts with long, black, spindly spider legs.

12

Burn, Baby Burn. Disco Spider Inferno!

Asher

JJ's screaming like a six-year-old little girl. I hear his voice get deeper as he yells my name. I'm on the other side of the club, with the bar between us. He is near the exit, hollering and pointing.

I look in the direction of his dainty finger, and I pee a little bit.

Yup, that's definitely pee.

One of the clusters of disco balls cracks open and separates. Four spindly legs pop out of each hole. Eight eyes emerge in the center, each with a hideously bright gold pupil. Little fangs protrude from under the mass of eyes, and I pee a little more.

Goddamn Disco Spiders. The size of horses. Are you fucking serious? There are so many, it's impossible to count. Others see them too and start screaming while they run for the exits.

Oh, that's why JJ was near the exit. He's so smart.

The spiders break from their clusters and aim for the doorways, stomping on people in their way. One sharp leg lances right through a man's eye. He dangles from the leg as the spider keeps walking and rears up before it shoots a web out of its abdomen, covering the front entrance and a group of shrieking people. Panic sets in as clubbers start screaming, trying to find other ways out. I look around and find the other exits are blocked too.

People get caught in web sprays, slamming them up against doors and parts of the upper level. A diligent spider swathes muted human shapes like leftovers, wrapping them up like white cigar cocoons. You can see their bodies wiggling beneath, weakly trying to fight for air, going limp like flies caught in their trap.

The music comes to a stop—finally—as a giant spider climbs up into the DJ booth and attacks the ginger DJ who has been assaulting our ears for the last few hours. The soulless disc jockey tries to avoid the spider's attacks by smacking at it with his laptop. The beast bobbed and weaved before it leapt upon the redhead's back as he turned to run. The fangs hook into the pasty DJ's eyes over his head, eliciting a scream that chills my bones. A vile crunch erupts as the spider pulls back and rips the crown of his skull off creating a geyser of blood and chunks, making the DJ platform topple over in the commotion.

Ducking down and looking for my bestie, I spot him standing on one of the tables with a barstool in hand, battling off one of the spiders. He looks like a lion-tamer in a circus, trying to shoo lions away. Just with more flair. JJ lands a blow to the spider, knocking its body hard with the legs of the stool. A high-pitched wail emanates from its mouth, and other Saturday Nightmare Fever fuckers come running. *(Spiders....duh)*

I'm so proud of my ride-or-die. Welp, maybe not die. He bougie. More like he's gonna have a lot of smart-ass questions, and then he'll help me figure out how not to die. I shake my head because I can get lost in my own sarcasm and humor at the worst time. I mean, I am a funny bitch.

SEE? I almost did it again. -Ok, back to us saving the day, er night.

Watching the dynamic diva, who had become like family to me, battling one of his worst fears, mine disappears. I will fuck these overgrown arachnoid hoes up. I run around the bar and grab a tall bottle of Ciroc. I make a face at it.

Ain't this Diddy The Diddlers shit? Fuck it.

Running as fast as my thick thighs can, I make a run for the spider. It pays no attention to me as I jump off an overturned booth and dive on that mother fucker, bottle raised. It cracks across the spider's carapace and shatters, slamming the giant hissing beast down to the ground. I take the jagged piece of the bottle neck and jab it into the eyes of the spider and twist.

It makes a high-pitched scream. Another one within earshot stops eating some preppy-looking silver fox and turns toward us. Before it can make a move, a werewolf in a familiar-looking orange dress tears into it with massive razor-sharp claws.

What the fuck? A Werewolf?

"JJ, are you seeing this too? Or am I losing it? I literally fought a zombie that came out the goddamn mirror and brought a fucking desert with it. Don't get me started on the bird bitch. I need to know what I'm seeing is what I am actually seeing," I retort.

"I didn't hear half of what you said over the screams of the dying, but bitch, yes. I see it too. Not that orange, though, that's a fall color. It's August."

He was clubbing a downed spider beast into the ground.

"Don't get me started on the shit I've been seeing. My therapist is going to have to play a drinking game every time I say "oooooh bitch.""

JJ jumps off a table, almost falling into my arms, and even though I'm little, my ass is mighty, so I help steady him. A million thoughts and emotions are swirling through my head, but I don't have time to process them while I watch the big dick Minotaur come to life. The shock is cut short as two ladies, an older woman with silver streaks and a pale, over bleached blonde run past him screaming.

The monster's outstretched massive hand clamps onto the pale one and with his other he brings his axe down upon the silver fox. Blood sprays her still-surviving friend, coating the pasty crone in a crimson sheen as she tries not to swallow what landed in her mouth.

The big dick Minotaur, still gripping her screaming head-damaged hair, swings her up and into the air, like she weighs nothing. She spins a few times before she hits the glass ceiling, splatting like a dead bug. However, what goes up must come down. When the squashed potato body peeled off the ceiling, she became impaled right on one of those giant fucking horns. Glistening intestines wrap around the massive tine as gravity pulls her down. He shakes his head like an angered dog trying to loosen it, continuing to thrash until bits of bitch surround him.

Turning to JJ, I holler, "We need to get through those webs and get the fuck out of here!"

JJ has been watching the minotaur massacre with a devilish grin on his face, when he turns and looks at the nearest exit. He answers with his "nuh uh girl" face, looking at the tunnels of webbing and what may lie within them.

"There has to be another way out of this bitch!" I say, seeing no other viable ways. "And where the fuck is Dorian?"

"Bruh, this is all his fault. Everything. I knew I should have kept my ass at home. The ancestors said, 'Stay your ass home and don't date a colonizer.' They're probably laughing their asses off right now."

He lets out a long sigh and flips his bay-yang. Looking around the Clurb, it's something out of a horror movie. Maybe a B movie, but still horror.

The animated Lamia statue has twisted her serpentine lower half around a group of screaming clubbers, trapped and trying to tear through the webs that block the patio door. In one pull, each one of their faces contorts in agony. Two guys' faces are so red it looks like they'd been out in the sun for ten hours. The monstrous Lamia cackled as she swirls her body, tightening her grip until their bodies crackle and stretch from the pressure, and their heads explode. Pieces of broken skulls and brains shower the area, resembling scrambled eggs in ketchup, coating the monster bitches golden scales.

A blur speeds past me again. I can't make out anything but red glowing eyes as it takes flight, diving like a bird of prey onto the back of one of the disco spiders. Now that the blur stopped moving at that inhuman speed, I see it's the pretty light-skinned girl in the black lace from earlier.

Our eyes meet from across the room. She bears sharp fangs, digging them into the spider's back. Her throat bobs up and down, swallowing the spider's blood. When she pulls her mouth away from the downed monster, she wipes the blood from her mouth, and her eyes ignite in the darkened club. In a flash, she flies back up into the darkened club rafters.

JJ pulls me behind a downed table.

"I have had it with these motherfucking monsters in this motherfucking club!" JJ yells. "Vampires too?!"

I peek around the other side.

"Wait, wait, wait now. The Mariah Carey-looking one is pretty as hell. I'd let her bite me any day."

"You still remain the only thing making me believe bisexuals are real. But can you please keep it in your pants, at least until we make it out of here?"

"PANSEXUAL! How many times do I have to tell you? We all know bisexual people are a myth. Pan is where it's at."

"We are going to get *so* canceled after this."

We both laugh until a clap of spider guts hits the sideways tabletop, snapping us back to reality. We watch a group of people run around us, fighting things we can't see, while others fall prey to the spiders.

"There are too many of them. We need something that will take them out quickly." He says as he looks around for the closest weapon with a worried expression, creating lines on his face where they shouldn't be.

An idea slaps me on my booty, and I grin as I reach into my tiddies.

"Girl, we are in public, and people can see you."

"Let 'em look."

A wicked grin lights up his face.

"You have something up your tiddy, don't you?"

"You know it, bitch."

Finally wrapping my hands around the hard plastic, I pull out my *Vampire Blood Bath and Body Works spray.*

JJ covers his nose, "bitch, you better not have pooted. Not right now, I can only take so much."

I hold back my guilty giggle. It was just a little poot. I reach back in and pull out my pink Bic lighter.

"Body spray alone may not be able to cause enough damage, but fucking fire can."

"All you had to do was grab one of the damn liquor bottles bitch!"

"No. It's always body spray that saves the day! Haven't you read the first two books of this series?"

He rolls his eyes at me.

"Read and reviewed and even drew the new cover, belovedT."

I run up to the nearest spider, ducking its thrashing arms before I pump twice and flick my lighter. A beautiful mist of fire lights the mother fucker up.

JJ picks up a bottle of Hennessy from off the bar.

"I am not allowed to drink that. Henny makes me wanna fight mother fuckers," I say.

Shut the fuck up, Asher. We fighting for our fucking lives.

"It tastes like ass anyway, and I know what ass tastes like." He says as he lobs it at the spider. It shatters, the dark intoxicating liquid adding more fuel for the hungry flames.

I smile at my bestie and we watch as the beast backpedals, trying to run from the fire, but it's no use because it IS the fire.

It falls against the wall and sets the other booths ablaze. Flames lick up the walls, dancing towards Dorian's shrouded portrait, igniting one of the laser machines that explodes, rocking the entire club. I can't stop staring at the eyes behind the shroud, which feel like they're staring a hole in me.

"This bitch is going to go up with us inside if we don't find a way out of here!" he yells as I peek around the side to see if the coast is clear.

The overgrown spiders are attacking the vivified monsters and vice versa. The chaos dissipates as more mangled bodies hit the ground. The few surviving beasts are barely visible through the shrouded depths of webbed corridors.

I whip my head around and who do I see, but our beloved fancy, double-dipping fucktart of a boyfriend behind the bar. I can see him accessing a hidden panel located behind a section of the liquor shelves.

"Oh, now he wants to show up?" I say with an emotional sneer.

I watch as the panel opens and a giant red button appears. He slams his hand on it, and a sprinkler system whirs to life. I prepare myself to get rained on, blinking as I look above me when the only sprinkler located above the portrait case mists the area down. JJ joins me in watching all this unfold, when we see a short blonde man in a blue suit appear out of thin air.

Suit says something to Dorian's cheating ass and I hear him shouting, "The fire department means the cops come next!"

Dorian looks like a disheveled ball of stress. "Wow, and people say I'm vain?" JJ says beside me.

"His whole club is about to become one big insurance claim, and he's worried about a painting?"

JJ backs up to the wall behind us, grabbing a golden mace as long as a bat that came loose from the explosion.

"I can't speak on skewed priorities-" he says as he hands me a golden dagger he plucked off the wall.

"But he's got bigger problems to worry about right now."

We throw the table out of our way and charge towards the bar.

"Are you ready to sink with your ship, old man?"

I yell out as I take a swing with this heavy sum-bitch at the pair.

I know it's only a dagger, but I got lil' lady hands.

The golden sword lands with a thunk on the bar top, shocking both of the dapper douchebags. Attempting to pull it loose, Blue Suit hyperspeed shoulders me and sends me sprawling to the ground. Before I even stop rolling, JJ comes in and hits a home run across the ghoul's chest with the mace. My head stops spinning just in time to see it connect, rocking the vampire up against the bar. His back snaps back as a gargled scream exits his mouth.

Dorian, stunned, yells out,

"What the fuck?! How do you even know each other?!"

He gets cut off by the sound of scuffling.

"Igor! You fucking piece of shit!"

JJ yells, as he's already standing over *Igor,* cranking up for another swing.

"You don't," Igor kept rolling.

"Hit a lady," Igor ducked.

"Even if," Igor backed up enough and tried to stand.

"She's like, if a lady were also an uncle!"

JJ stepped closer and swung at his knee, cracking it into the other in a sickening crunch.

"He's healing way too fast," JJ yelled out in my direction. "I can only keep beating that ass for so long."

The hobbled vampire howled on the ground, crying tears of blood as JJ dropped the mace and grabbed him.

"Can you get Prettyboy?" JJ yelled out to me as I rolled away from the spreading flames and got my bearings.

"I'll deal with Igor's bitch ass." The pained, angry man wailed in JJ's shaking hands,

"My name isn't even Igor."

"Yeah, I suck at names," JJ said as he grabbed the back of Whatever-His-Name's head and clamped his gaping jaw onto the bar, holding it in place as he grabbed for his mace.

Dorian screamed, "WAIT!" just as I was cornering him. "Just let me explain!"

A blur of motion came hurtling towards the bar. When it came to a stop, the pair of baddies from earlier were standing between JJ and me. He let go of Not-Igor, holding the mace up in front of him in protection. Not-Igor's jaw stayed in place. The shiny golden mace looked ready to curb check him one last time.

"That's not going to kill him," the thicc one, now with long black hair and body poured into a hot pink dress, said as her eyes reflected in the dark space. "But it would be fun to watch."

JJ looked at her, then me, weighed his options for 1.2 seconds before the bloodied blue suit vampire whirled, exposing his fangs at all of us. JJ swung the gold spiked mace and caught Not-Igor in the mouth with a muffled, crackly crunch. Blood, a few teeth, and a fang spray Dorian in his stunned face. The rest of the vampire's teeth washed down his gurgling mouth as he slumped to the ground.

The two girls whooped and clapped, my Mariah Carey wifey grabbed the mace from JJ's hand and dragged Not-Igor's quivering body away from the bar.

"We'll finish this one off, do you all got Prettyboy?" she asked, her voice dripping with sex.

Whew.

"He won't be so pretty once I get my hands on him," I growl as I finally pull the golden sword free.

"Just be careful, he's more dangerous than he looks." My wifey warns us before her Thickly in Pink friend joins her, and they drag Not-Igor at a blurring speed. *What exit did they use?*

Dorian continues to stammer with his back against the literal wall, the ground shakes, and the hardwood below our feet begins to creak and splinter.

"What the fuck, man!" JJ yells out, "There's more?!"

13

OK, Boomer

Phrique

I'm caked in blood. You know, again. For real this time. Haven't I suffered enough? I hold my mace at the ready, watching Asher's back as a screech unlike anything I've ever heard comes from the back hall that's now a lint trap of gore-dotted spider webs. On the other side of the bar, the flames are licking the ceiling. A few pieces of the rafters have started to fall, and I know we don't have that much time left. The club was dark now, with only minimal light coming from the fires and the outside lighting. This is the one time I miss the fucking lasers to light a way for us. Unfortunately, the ceiling inferno had already cooked the various laser projectors. One or two lay on their sides, flashing dimly in the distant corners.

I look across the ice rink of blood and body parts that used to be the dance floor for any other exit that isn't barred with web. Four pairs of glowing red orbs emerge from the gauze-strewn chasm, and I let out the manliest scream I can muster.

"We are getting SO McSued! It's the motherfucking Queen! Or the mother! Or whatever!" I yell as I take off in the opposite direction, aiming to grab Asher.

"It's the big ass motherfucking spider from IT, dammit!" I scream, pulling Asher from her revenge-drunk focus.

Dorian is holding his profusely bleeding arm on his knees, begging for his life. I hate to interrupt him being right where we want him, but...motherfuckin' big ass spider.

Asher's head whirls to me, and I watch her eyes grow wider *(how is that possible??)* as she looks past and just above my head.

"I see it too! Gotdamn, that's a huge bitch!" She yells as she steps away from Dorian with her jaw still agape.

"Let that fuckboi be spider food!" I yell as I motion with a nod towards the outside patio area.

"Let's go smoke! Let's go smoke!" She follows my lead toward the double doors, when a revoltingly loud *hawk tua* noise echoes behind us.

A beam of milky white web flies past us, catching Dorian off guard, pinning him against the bar as whatever leftover bottles crash around him. He screams out as the beady-eyed arachnid closes the distance between them. Asher and I get to the double doors. I'm kicking and dragging the bodies out of the way to clear a path to the doorway as Asher is whacking away at the sticky web. She's making some progress, but most of the silk is sticking to the blade like gooey cotton candy.

We both turn when we hear Dorian yelling and begging for his life. The monstrous spider is now in plain sight. It's easily the size of a tank and looks just as heavy. Even in the low lighting, you can see its legs pounding holes in the hardwood as it stalks its prey. The mega disco ball above it still continues to spin and send small fractals of light that highlight its overgrown, hairy features. I can't help but watch between pulls of the webbing, so does Asher. Both of us wanted to at least see our ex—now spider fodder—get what he deserves, even if we couldn't do it ourselves. Plus, he's seen our O faces, and that does some shit to your psyche, I swear. Plus, I'm petty. It's one of my superpowers. It looks close enough to grab him—meaning we were next—but stops in its tracks as a moat of alcohol surrounds Dorian's web-encased jerking body.

The giant spider flinches back as the Long Island Iced Tea concoction snakes across the floor, flowing toward the direction of the fire. I was relieved, finally, something was going in our favor as we almost had the door clear.

> *Ex: who transgressed against us*
> *+ killer mutant spider*
> *+ fire*
> *= vengeance*
> *= WIN*

but then...

there was no closure in that equation.

> *Me*
> *+ Asher*
> *x (killer mutant spider + fire)*
> *divided by (Crispy Dorian)*
> *= no closure.*

Fuck.

Also, *fuck math.*

"Dorian and Charlotte *(it seemed fitting)* are about to go up in flames," I say to Asher, wiping the sweat from my brow.

"Good riddance, 'bout time we got a break in this damned story." Asher said, sluggishly letting the sword drop.

"We won't ever find out what the hell happened here tonight or why he was such a hoe and lied to us," I say, with a pang of regret in my voice.

"I can let it go if you can."

"No, you can't," Asher said, resting her hands on her knees before she stood up tall(-ish).

"Let's kill that big bitch."

We crept back towards the bar, ducking between downed tables, human, and arachnid detritus, so we didn't get noticed. Once close enough, I looked around for anything I could do to stop this impending explosion. Out of nowhere, a groan comes from one of the heaps of bodies. A lone survivor is crawling across the floor in our direction, to our vexation.

"Damn, why does that loud bitch gotta bring that shit over here?" We both whisper at the same time, best/worst timing ever.

The mangled form of a club ho, gets within arm's reach of us, and a cannonball of web collides with and rockets them across the room. The wad of limbs and hair extensions adheres to the wall next to Dorian's still encased painting, hampering some of the flames with a sickening hiss and crackle.

My eyes lit up, then immediately dropped back into a roll.

"I know what to do," I whisper to Asher, mapping out the space between us and the rising flames. Unfortunately, I've played this video game scenario before.

"What? Tell me the plan." She whispers back, wincing at the sticky remains stuck to the wall like tree sap on a windshield.

"Just get to Dorian if you can, cut him free. I have to distract that big bitch. Ok?"

"Fuck," she says, looking back to where she left her sword a few feet away. "I really need to get high after all this."

"Tell you what, if we live after all this, maybe I'll even give the devil's lettuce a try. I can cross it off my bucket list after *killing a big ass spider.*"

"Oh, I'm going to get you high as shit." She said with an excited whisper, "We got this. Just be careful."

"If I don't make it, promise me they'll throw my ashes in the eyes of my enemies," I say, adrenaline flooding my system as I get ready to make this sprint. "Especially that bad-built Barbie ex-admin of that horror book group that tried to get my brown ass blacklisted and failed porcelain-ly."

Asher starts to tear up.

"I'm just being dramatic. Let's kill this bitch." I conclude before we both take off in opposite directions.

Running, screaming with my hands waving above my head, past the fire. As expected, '*Charlotte*' spat more globs of web at me. Each loogie slapped and spread across the walls and floor on impact, putting out the biggest sources of the flames.

If I circled back once more, I might be able to get them all, but I wasn't sure if I wanted to chance dodging the sticky clumps on the floor. Could this get any more revolting? I shudder.

I look back to make sure the mega-spider was staying far enough away from Asher. '*Charlotte*' gave up going after Dorian, so Asher was in the clear. The colossal creepy-crawly seemed to be getting restless. No matter how many times I ran or ducked, it wouldn't leave the center of the space or get near any of the flammable liquid spilling around the club. My beautiful brain was officially out of ideas now that I was almost out of floor space. When I peered from hiding behind the remnants of a booth, a beam of light reflected, annoyingly, off the oversized disco ball above us, right into my eye. *AGAIN.* The annoyance quickly melts as I finally figure out how to beat this final boss.

A gob of spider sputum rocks the back of the booth, spraying bits of goo on my arms and shoulders that I wriggle free from. I run to the single laser projector in the corner, burning my fingers as I flip that hot bitch upright and point it up at the disco ball. I crank the laser setting up to maximum output, heavy strobe; forever thankful that

Dorian's boomer ass never opts for the WiFi/Bluetooth models.

As planned, the darkened space is awash in a galaxy of pink and turquoise rays of light, multiplied a few hundred times over. The prisms of color dance over all eight eyes of the eight-legged freak, discombobulating it. Distracting it long enough to be able to run full speed ahead towards Asher before I yelled,

"Hand me my sword, ho!"

The chaotic outburst jolted everyone in the room, but Asher picked up what I was putting down and threw it my way. I caught it and felt like I was firing on all cylinders. I zeroed in on the steel cable securing the shining beacon of disco destruction to the D-ring and readied the tacky, *tacky* sword, praying it was sharp enough. I had to keep the angered arachnid's overtaxed eyes on me, so I yelled out *Parkoouurrr!* as I summoned the final stretch of my zoomies. Feeling the vibrations of the oversized garden pest petulantly pound the floor behind me as I bounded up on the bar top and slashed at the exposed steel cable with all my might.

Asher's head jerked from my movements to the impending carnage, yelling out, "Ohhh shiiittt!"

There was a spark and a roar as the metals clashed, followed by the whir and snap of the mega-sized mirror ball crashing down on the gigantic cobweb creator. They both exploded in a duet of glittering gore. The pre-contaminated space reverberated with eardrum-shattering echoes of squelching staccato slaps, as a torrent of crimson clapped against the walls and the poor souls below me. I closed my eyes and looked away as hot chunks of king-sized sloppy joe meat battered against me. The force and the stench of dehydrated fish carcasses reconstituted in microwaved garbage juice almost knocked me off the bar.

I wiped as much of the spider stew out of my eyes, nervous that the only noise I heard was angry drips from the ceiling meeting the gentle laps of the glistening red pond below it.

I turned to look around the darkened space; the only light source was the single laser projector pointing up at the empty, spattered ceiling. All the little flames got extinguished in the impromptu downpour. Giant gobs of Kool-Aid-stained web started to drop from the ceiling. *Who knew spider blood could dissolve spider web?*

The web shot that coated most of the burning wall sloughed off in one wet sheet that slumped and fell to the floor in a wet smack. It sent a wave of frothing blood and limbs in my direction, gently swaying Asher's supine, floating body toward me. Her body slowly pinwheeled and came to a stop with her eyes bulging, staring up at the ceiling.

"Oh shit! Asher!" I yell out, distress straining my vocal cords. I almost busted my ass trying to maneuver my way down off the bar to save her.

"Answer me! Are you okay?!"

She answers instantly, her eyes unblinking.

"I'm very much *not* okay, JAY JAY!" She said, *slightly perturbed* as she sat up creakily, dribbling god-knows-what off her. I exhale a huge sigh of relief as I fussily try to pull the nearest barstool to me with my shoe, *like a lady.*

"You couldn't warn a bitch first!" She hacked. "Or pulled a bitch up with you?!" she said as I safely landed. She gasped, looking down at her body, causing me to rush across the skating rink of stank awfulness to her aid, almost *eating it* on the coagulating floor.

"I have spider guts in my tiddies!" She yells in a shrill *(for her)* whine.

I stop in my tracks and wrinkle my nose. She fishes her pink lighter out of the punch bowl of prickly pieces—that is now her cleavage—and tests the flint. After a few tries, it creates a successful glowing flame, to her relief. I'm so happy she's alive, but I'm still kinda stuck with my eyes crinkled, nose wrinkled, and a downturned mouth...making *the face.*

"HELP ME, YOU BITCH!" She yells, thrusting her arms up in my direction.

I snap out of it and pull her up, overwhelmed with emotion. Even though I don't *do* hugs *(readers excluded!)*, I've never felt the need to hug someone so much in my life as I do right now. To let her know I care; that I would be lost without her; to tell her everything will be copacetic now that we are reunited, ready to take over the world together.

The thing is...she is like *sopped* in it. Like, there are hairy bits just *caked* on her. I don't have the heart to tell her an antenna or something crunchy-looking is stuck to her ass. Not to mention the-

She looks me in the face like she wants to kill me, then she pulls me in for a hug, and I let out a little sob. Accepting the embrace with open arms, doing my best not to breathe through my nose. I keep the bile down for the first few seconds. *Just for her.*

"Can we take Wanda—the fuck—home, please?" I say, pulling away from her, still fighting *the face.*

She gives me that knowing glare, then looks behind me to the bar.

"What about his ass?" Asher says, pointing toward it before she digs in her crunchy cleavage again and fishes out her cigarettes.

We saunter over to Dorian. He's coming to and noticing he's web-free but soaked in platelet punch. With a horrified face, he startles and backs up against the bar before he wipes his face and wails,

"I curse the day I ever laid eyes on you!"

We both chuckle.

"Which one?"

Asher lights her cigarette, and I raise my eyebrow. We part and stand on either side of the bar so he has no chance of escape. Dorian attempts to stand, sliding and grunting uncomfortably. He finally makes it upright when he slips and his forehead bounces off the shiny bar top. He catches himself, but his head volleys back as a gash blooms right between his eyes. We both step closer, our eyes trained on the wound as he yowls like a cat at three a.m. The blood drips off his nose. Sure enough, the skin pulled tight and started to slowly knit itself back together.

"So, do you want to start explaining? Or do you want me to open that back up every five minutes?" I say, doing my best to remain stoic. "I got time today."

"If we cut your dick off, will it still grow back crooked?" Asher said, exhaling her smoke and gutterally cackling.

"Pfftttt," I sputtered, trying to stay serious.

"I didn't hear you complaining," Dorian said snidely, wiping the blood from his face with a rag from behind the bar. "And there's no smoking in here. I-"

"Mother fucker, don't make me hop this bar." Asher seethed, keeping her cool and ashing her cigarette in a provocatively grand gesture.

"I wasn't complaining because I didn't know that I was dating Britain's Biggest Bisexual Man-Hoe!"

"Dammit." I said, deep in thought.

Asher and Dorian both turn to me, concerned.

"There's no word for slutbag manwhore fuckface that starts with a B. That would have been a nice combo." I say, shaking my head.

Asher and Dorian paused, thought about it, then looked back at me contemptuously, after a beat.

"Can you ever, for the life of you, EVER just—*NOT*?" Dorian says, his voice upspeaking.

Oh, he mad.

"Ever what?" I say, looping the proverbial noose & flipping my gotdamned hair for maximum cogency.

"Ever just...not be THIS. All this. This perpetual prince circus act. You dismissive, pompous, arrogant, man-child." He spat with a sneer.

I smirk wryly and run my tongue over my teeth.

"Didn't hear you complaining about any of that while you were bobbing on my knob like corn on the cob and eating my ass for a good ten minutes." I retorted, before I popped my tongue.

Asher choked and coughed up plumes of tobacco smoke, cackling between coughing fits and grasping her knees.

"JAY JAY!" Her yell echoed around us. "EW!"

She stood upright again.

"Hey, wait," she said, deep in thought, before she painfully suppressed it. She turned to Dorian and yelled,

"Dorian! Why did you lie to us?"

Dorian looked legitimately hurt and taken aback.

"My dear sweet, naive, pugnacious Asher, when have I ever lied to you?"

"JJ!" She didn't take her eyes off him. "Did this bitch just call me a damn dog?!" Asher yelled.

"Can we just kill his ass?!" She lunged at Dorian, making him flinch before he slipped and fell back onto the blood-slicked interior of the bar. He let out a string of expletives as Asher and I advanced on him.

"Why were you fucking us both, Dorian?!" She yelled in his direction as he begrudgingly tried to stand.

"Fucking," he grunted and waved a broken bottle around in front of him.

"Besides a serious lapse in judgment." He winced, displaying his hand hanging limply at a sick angle from his forearm toward us. Implying fault; assigning blame; soliciting sympathy. Our faces stayed deadpan. I glanced at my watchless, *intact* wrist, then back at him.

"I THOUGHT WE WERE POLY! FUCK!" He yelled as his bones crackled and popped ever-so-slowly, back in place.

Asher and I turned to each other with arms akimbo and pursed our lips before we scoffed and looked back at him.

"When were you going to tell us about it?" We both furiously replied in unison.

Dorian's eyes watered as his compound fracture popped back in his ragged skin with a nauseating slurp.

"Are you going to keep killing me until sunup? Or just when the cops get here and find you both, covered in blood, in a club, full of DEAD PEOPLE." Dorian spat out.

His voice echoed through the damp space. Asher looked around the grisly scene through a wide-eyed, objective perspective.

"I don't know," I said, giving Dorian a skeptical look.

"I think I heard that fake British accent kinda falter a bit."

I stare incredulously at him as I fish my phone out of my pocket, silently surprised that it was still intact.

"Anyhoo, as much as I hate being a Karen, we can just call the cops and get this all over with." I looked toward Asher, unlocking my phone.

"Philanderer. Killer. Gaudy gold glutton. Date rapist? Plus, he wanted to do the spit in my mouth thing and just...gross."

"Hey, wait," Asher piped up. "I think I taught him that one."

I winced.

"That's fine, I taught him the tongue thing. You're welcome, by the way."

"How on earth am I a date rapist?" Dorian yelled irritably.

"All this!" I yell out. Motioning to the club full of body parts and gelatinous gore.

"Whatever fucking drug you made with Igor-, sorry, Not-Igor and put in our drinks! Does consent mean nothing to your generation? The 1800s or whatever?"

"Gross. How old are you?" Asher piped up, sending waves of ageism threateningly around her.

"Lotus was-" He paused to think.

"It was in the VIP bracelets. It was a FREE party favor. I gave you FREE DRUGS. You-" Dorian rubbed his sinuses and let out a deep exhale.

"I don't know what went so wrong. All it was supposed to do was manifest your deepest desires. It was supposed to be absinthe and orgies! Good, clean fun. Not slaughter an entire club full of people! Not turn my beautiful golden palace into a disco bloodbath!"

I gave a nod of approval. Nice reference.

"Wait. Wait. Wait. What do you mean by drinks?" he asked, suspiciously.

"The glow in the dark drinks that golden Dita Von Teese lookin' girl gave us. The ones that were *weak AF* by the way." Asher yelled, huskily.

Dorian looked at us dubiously, flourishing his broken bottle towards us again.

"Glow in the-" he spoke with a parched mouth.

"She gave you the-" He looked at us and shook angrily.

"She gave you the Nectar of Ambrosia?!" He exclaimed, blinking slowly before he threw himself on the bar.

"...I've made a *huge* mistake," he uttered under his breath.

"Girl, that's an understatement. You gave people an untested drug, and all but *TWO* of them are *DEAD*. You are going to spend your immortality–or whatever your stupid mutant power is–in jail. Unless we like, cut you in half and bury the halves on two different continents."

Asher gave me a nod of approval. *That was a good idea.*

"I didn't kill them, you judgmental, hypocritical, egomaniac!" He said through clenched teeth, sweating as he looked around.

"It was your fucked up brains who created these nightmare scenarios that came to life. Even your unlocked inhibitions are weird and outlandish. Fucking horror authors. Why did it have to be edgelord splatterpunk authors?!"

Asher and I put our heads together and yelled "Link in bio!" out of habit, visibly ashamed.

"And stop fucking smoking in here!" Dorian yelled, lobbing a bloody bottle of tequila toward us.

Asher and I parted just as it sailed between us and hit the back wall. Liquor and broken glass exploded behind us. Our eyes met. I gave her the *welp* face.

"Alright, I'd say it's about time we wrap this up. Let's get Grandpappy to bed."

I cautiously stepped closer to Dorian, motioning for Asher to go around the other way. Asher caught the end of my hand gesture and quickly blew her smoke out before she flicked her cigarette butt behind her.

"ASHER WAI-" I yell, my eyes as big as dinner plates.

"Oh shit!" she yelled, bounding away from where the glowing cherry bounced into the liquor puddle.

The flames reignited, engulfing the already structurally compromised wall with the teetering plexiglass case that housed Dorian's aged painting. His eyes frenzied, dancing between us and his precious covered portrait. We watched him closely as he flung his body to the other side of the bar, tapping the same button previously. The sprinkler above wheezed and moaned, but stayed dormant to Dorian's vexation.

"Your pretty picture is the least of your worries, Mr. Belvedere," I say, keeping my eyes on him as I edge closer to my golden mace, shimmering from the light of the flames.

"Your references always give away your real age, you know," he said, shaking his head.

"But I guess that doesn't...matter anymore," Dorian said, with sweat pouring off his face and soaking his shirt as he tried to locate Asher.

I grabbed the mace by the handle and looked toward the blackening plexiglass case behind me.

"Hey Asher, I wonder what would happen if I broke this case open," I say, winking at her.

She stepped back, away from the bar, toward me, and Dorian instantly flinched.

Got'eem.

The shroud within the case falls off the portrait, igniting within the steaming plexiglass. The face staring back at us is a hideous, demonic rictus of repulsion that burned itself into our minds.

Asher breaks away from the mesmerizing gaze before she shakes her head and laughs.

"So that's it? That's the big reveal?" Asher says, leaning down to grab the golden dagger. It glinted in her hand.

"Can I take a whack at the piñata first?" She said, positioning herself just outside of the range of the fire.

"Wait! Wait! If you do, you'll-" Dorian paused, stepping outside of the bar with his arms extended out toward us.

"I can still help you. I can show you how to-"

"How to what? How to get trapped in a picture to get roasted by some baddies?" Asher says, sticking out her tongue.

"Owwww! How to fumble the ball? Fumble the bag?" I yell, cackling.

Dorian dropped to his knees, his feet turning to blackened charcoal, smoking behind him. His face twisted in anguish.

"How to make the pact," he yelps in pain, "to stay young and beautiful forever. You fools!"

"Wait a minute," I say as my mental record skips.

"I've heard about these. I can keep my boyish good looks if I just make a deal with the White devil. Right?"

Asher stopped in the middle of a giggle,

"Wait, JJ. Wait, wait, wait. You don't need that. You–You-you still look good."

"Ah, that hesitation though," I say, contemplating if it actually does get *greater* later.

We jump when the pipes above us groan and sputter, spitting out a shower of water that drips onto the flames into oblivion. Dorian heavily sighs before falling over and staring at his salvaged painting.

"Talk about dumb luck." I shake my head and look down at him.

"So what is it, Dorian? A transfer? Signed in blood? My firstborn? Then what, whatever happens to my picture happens to me?"

Relieved, he spoke.

"A pact. A transfer. Just a simple wish. You'll live forever." He winced, looking back at his legs as smoke still puffed from within his shoes.

"It's still on fire! Oh fuck! It's smoldering!" he winced, crawling closer to the blackened burn marks.

"Oh shit!" I yell, swinging the mace at it, only for it to ricochet off and vibrate down to my toes.

"Fuck," I say, looking to Asher for help. She's looking at me like I've lost my fucking mind. I flip my hair and give her a wink, to her stunned surprise.

"Dorian!" I pop up as tears fill his eyes.

"Can it be any picture? Even your commission? Can you make another pact and use that?"

He paused to think, looking up at his reflection in the tinted ceiling.

"I-I have no choice, but I'm not going to make it to your place in time," he said as his flesh sizzled and popped.

I shake my head and smirk.

"Ok, Boomer." I laugh and pull out my phone again.

"It's 2025. Everything is on the cloud."

After a few taps, I pull his commissioned art piece up and present it to him.

His tears continue to drip down his face, as it begins to darken and blister. Dorian looks at the commission, then at me ever so grateful that I am so forgiving and opportunistic. *I'm certainly one of those things.*

"Do your thing PeePaw," I say, holding my phone out to face him.

He quivers beneath me. His age is showing. He stares at his face and starts to mouth silent words. I can see my art reflected in his glassy eyes. Electricity flows around us. I can see Asher's shoulders tensing up as she watches for any invisible enemies closing in. The air goes cold before pulling through me, chilling my bones until I can feel it moving through my fingertips.

Dorian lets out an exhausted exhale, feebly mumbling.

"No mortal eye must ever see it," he murmured, "The truth."

Asher watched the encased portrait go ashen and dissolve into crumbling dust. She turned to me, nervously watching us both.

"Yeah, yeah, yeah. Super secret. It's in the vault." I say as I turn the screen to me.

My beautiful art has morphed into a disturbing image of plague and decay. The full-body piece I created now shows a tumorous creature whose eyes damn anyone who looks into them. Black death stares through me, breathing its pestilence into every cell of my being. The contagions crystallize in my joints as I bring my finger to my screen.

Each tap aches. I tear my soul back from the demonic gaze and blink the horrors away.

"Hey Asher, check your texts."

"Got it. Posted."

"Gracias," I say, glancing down at Dorian's aghast face.

He attempts to crawl away from us, still weakened and pale.

"Be a doll and post it to Splatterpunk Society, too, please."

"Done and done." She chimes in,

"I can make a TikTok with it. Start the #DorianGray-Challenge and see how far it goes."

"Bless that horrible app," I say,

"Godspeed."

Dorian's bloodshot eyes are damning me and every-thing I've ever loved with his death stare. I shrug my shoulders in mock innocence.

"Opposite Day?"

He lunges toward me. His knees crackle against the tacky floor, and the defeat begins to register on his face as he glares up at me.

"Hell has room," he utters as he takes a swing at me.

"Keep it warm for me, Daddy."

I pull away, keeping my phone out of his reach when my thumb accidentally swipes the screen. A vile crackle breaks the jovial air, followed by a gurgling scream that erupts from Dorian's mouth. The jarring emissions shook us both as we recoiled, staring at his elbow bent backward in a grotesque display. I tear away from the sickening spectacle to see Dorian's image, still open in my drawing app. The swipe added a thick black line through the arm in Dorian's commission.

"Oh shit," I whisper.

I tap undo, testing out a still-forming hypothesis. This removes the black line, but his limb stays bobbing and throbbing, pointing in the wrong direction. Dorian continued to shake and wail, looking away as the blood began to soak his white shirt sleeve.

"The TikTok already has 160 views, 22 shares."

Asher reports, distracting her from the deformity in front of her.

"Asher, come look at this," I say, opening layers and pondering what mischief we could crash this plane with.

She comes up behind me and peers over my shoulder. I zoom out of the image and tap on the hair layer, toggling it off. We both gasp and hoot as Dorian's trademark locks disappear and a shining, white, sniveling cueball stares back at us.

"Oh, honey, who knew your hair did so much work for you?" Asher said, snapping pictures from behind me. Dorian's whines turn to enraged beastly snarls. "Let me try."

We switch phones and I continue to share Dorian's new lewk, tagged, across all the major platforms with the caption, "*Wig flew to outer space.*"

It's getting all the laugh-reacts.

"What does this do?" Asher asked, jabbing at the screen helter-skelter.

She enabled multiple-layer-erase mode, waving the cursor over his feet and knees on screen. Dorian rocked back on his ass as a blood-curdling scream erupted from his throat. Synchronized with the app, his lower legs are completely obliterated. His off white bone shines like a full moon in a meaty sky, raining red in vibrant spurts. His blood paints the floor in an arc in front of him; a new coat to add to the dried spider jelly below it.

"Oh my damn," I say, grimacing.

The rusty bouquet of adrenaline-charged blood and Dorian's unleashed bowels sadly reinvigorated my sense of smell.

"Erase his mouth," I yell over his screams. "Before I get a migraine."

His clamoring had quieted. The uttered damnations he choked out made no sense. What little color his skin had appeared bleached, as his life force surrounded him, presenting him like a condemned man on a crimson platter. *His end was nigh.*

Asher tapped through his head layers and ham-handedly deleted his face folder. There was a pause in Dorian's aria of pain when he brought his only working hand to his translucent face. His quivering fingers caressed the bare ribbons of tendon and fat that had shaped his once-handsome face.

You know, if you go for the whole imposed Eurocentric standards of beauty thing.

"Sweet baby Jeebus," mumbled a stunned, nictitating Asher.

"Well, there's no going back after that."

"We are killing his ass, right?" Asher asked, scrolling through options.

The anguished moans continued from the wilting woman-and-man-izer as I surveyed the damage we had inflicted.

"He isn't healing at all. I think this is it."

"That's good, cuz I can't *wait* to get this bra off."

I make my TMI face. She giggles.

"How do I shove something up his ass?" Asher asks rapidly. "Where's his dick? Let's cut that off, too!" She laughs maniacally.

"I don't know if you can-" I say, looking at the catastrophe on my screen.

"I didn't draw his dick." I chuckled.

"Well, I'm done with it. It was fun while it lasted. You good?" She asked, with her finger hovering over the screen."

"Fuck it off," I say, preparing myself for sympathy pains from this impromptu gelding.

Asher swiped down and a cavity from Dorian's navel down to where his thighs met unbarred, unleashing wet spools of bubble gum pink innards with red sprinkles that slopped out from his *abbreviated* legs.

His final words are a whispered, "lesbian haircut," eliciting a single tear from my eye.

We watched in solemn victory as Dorian exhaled his final breath and the last of his sanguineous syrup bloomed from the chasm.

"Damn," I say.

We both shake our heads, and I pop my phone back in my pocket.

"Dick really is the root of all evil."

14

Werewolves and Vampires and Zaddies, Oh Myyyy!

Asher

I thought I knew Dorian. I thought he really saw me. I was convinced I knew the real him. The man under all the beauty, but none of that was real.

You think you can truly see inside someone, until you are *literally* staring at their *actual,* bloody insides.

Never again will I let a man, or anyone for that matter, come between me and my ride-or-die.

JJ likes to say he's not down for the die part, but tonight, he could have easily been killed. Instead, he swooped in and saved us both. I mean, a bitch did help, but I would probably be a spider sammich right now if it wasn't for him.

I watched him preening and checking his hair on any reflective surface he could find. Meanwhile, mine was deep-conditioned in spider-bits stew. I didn't even care that he looked almost perfect right now. What mattered-he was alive.

"Let's get the fuck out of here. And please do me a favor. Remind me that I'm a lesbian the next time you hear me mention a man, because I am officially done with dick."

"I've been telling you this for how long, and it takes a near-death experience for you to listen to me? I think being attracted to men is a mental illness. I know what I would choose if I had a choice." He looks around at something, *a camera perhaps?*

"Unfortunately, it isn't, cuz I sure as hell would wish better for myself."

He crosses his arms and rolls his eyes.

"Why are we still here?" I ask.

"I was looking for my backpack."

"JAY JAY, YOU HAVE EIGHTY MORE."

"ALRIGHT FINE."

His pout turns to revulsion as he sees me fishing things out of my tiddies.

"I think that was an eyeball," I mutter, tossing it aside before I cough again.

"I swear I swallowed some spider bits. I need to vomit and take a long ass shower."

"I'm not getting out of my bathtub all day tomorrow. Hold all my calls."

There's some kind of commotion up on the roof, reminding us that we may not be out of the disco woods just yet.

"Fuck this shit, let's go before the cops show up." I check which door has fewer *obstacles* in front of it.

"You know I don't fuck with one-time."

"ACAB" He adds, "Ladies first."

We have to avoid stepping on bodies, bits, and mirror shards as we make our way to the front of the house again. It's a huge fucking mess. It feels like we are running over rough mountain terrain. I avoid a torso and hop over someone's leg with a high heel attached. I can hear JJ moaning, groaning, and commenting on what a waste of good Louboutins.

The blood tsunami washed away the web that had once blocked us in this nightmare. It looks like Kool-Aid-soaked cotton candy but smells like hot buttered assholes in a burning outhouse. We work together to clear the broken furniture and body parts that stand between us and freedom. *Damn, I just wanna go home.*

Once it's all cleared, JJ kicks the door out, exposing way more than I needed to see of his undercarriage. They don't call them hoochie daddy shorts for nothing. The doors swing open. We do a quick check if the coast is clear before we *finally* step out of the wretched Club Hedonia.

The cool night breeze hits me, dancing through my gunky hair.

"I swear I ain't never been so happy to see the outside," I say, fishing for a cigarette.

"Chiiild, me-AAHHHHHH!" he shrieks mid-sentence as a creature cloaked in darkness falls from the sky and lands right in front of us.

To my surprise, it's the black lace beauty from before. I don't think JJ recognizes her right away; he's still screaming and punching the air with his eyes closed.

"Biiiiiitch!" I yell, before she turns and winks at me.

Another set of high heels clacks toward us. I turn to see the other hottie with the long black hair and phat ass coming our way.

"She does that shit to me all the time. I keep telling her, just because she can fly now doesn't mean she needs to be popping up in people's faces."

"What the fuck is happening? Are we still hallucinating shit?"

JJ finally opens his eyes and looks around,

"I see them too," he adds, his voice as raspy as mine now.

Serves him right.

Shawty in the black lace laughs.

"Nah, y'all ain't seeing shit, girl." Orange Dress speaks up.

"This is always a bit awkward, but considering it looks like you are well acquainted with our kind now...I'm Paris. I'm a werewolf. My girl Gina, she's a vampire."

I feel like they are fucking with us, but I remember seeing their eyes glowing before, but I thought I was just seeing shit. The image of the orange flash, taking a spider with it, came back to me. That was Paris; it all makes sense now.

"Dis tew much. Please tell me y'all weren't here because you were fucking Dorian too?" JJ spits.

"Naw babe, I'm a lesbian and Paris has a wife."

I swear to all that is gay, as soon as those words leave her lips, my panties re-moisten.

JJ responds to Gina, "Finally, someone with some sense around here," looking at me with concern, as I'm practically wiping the drool off my chin.

"Y'all still didn't answer the question, though."

My bestie had a bit of stank in his tone, but after what we had to deal with tonight, who could blame him? Plus, pretty bitches don't sway him one bit. He's a human bullshit detector. Most of the time. I on the other hand, my vagina has a mind of its own. *Don't blame me. Blame the pussy, because she is on fire right now, hunny.*

"I run a strip joint in Durham called Diamond Girls. Your man's assistant was there last weekend, telling my girls alllll his business. We run a supernatural community out there. Gina is just one of our many enforcers. She also has ties to other supernatural communities. Through networking, we have set up a list of "supes" that are the worst of the worst. When that guy mentioned Dorian Gray, the drug, and their plans, we took an interest. Pussy makes people talk."

Yup, she right.

JJ gives me a weird look while we listen to the girls. I can feel his eyes judging me.

"Dorian's ego, his lack of empathy, and his cruelty have been known to get others killed. He likes to corrupt and coerce people into being the worst versions of themselves. He has ruined countless lives." Paris continued.

"Bruh, this explains all the dairy he kept pushing on me. How diabolical." JJ says.

We all stare at him. The girls quickly learn that he just be sayin' shit sometimes.

"Anyways, thanks to you two, he won't be ruining anyone else's lives anymore," Gina said.

Paris added, "Yeah, I couldn't smell his scent, so I knew you guys got the upper hand on him. You figured out his weakness and lived to tell the tale."

JJ did a little bow.

"We owe y'all one." Gina professed and winked at me.

JJ beamed. Someone give this man a sticker. He turned to me again, waiting for some kind of signal that I was all good with a *wtf* expression.

Stop looking at me, dammit. I think I'm cumming.

"We used Lazarus, or what did you call him? Igor? Anyway, his assistant to get into Dorian's office. He kept it hidden and sealed off, only accessible from the roof. We've had to keep Lazarus alive long enough to use his fingerprint to open the door." Gina continued.

"Where is he now?" JJ asked, finally paying attention.

"Oh, he's strapped to the roof. He's got a hot date with the sunrise, which should be showing up pretty soon. He's going to pay for his crimes against his own kind." Gina said, shaking her head.

"We found stacks of incriminating evidence and this isn't the first time this has happened, unfortunately. We found all their files of the different drug experiments they created; this was just their first run. The file on Lotus contained valuable information. They used Kitsune blood, another supernatural creature. One we haven't encountered yet. It's like a fox with nine tails; their blood contains properties that can control human emotions, but with the wrong combination, it can make people hallucinate, in this case- their worst fears. Kitsune blood is rare; it ain't supposed to be used that way. They kidnapped one, held her captive, and bled her dry."

"So if it only tapped into our individual fears, why did everyone see the spiders?" I asked.

"Girl, everyone hates spiders," JJ said. "It's one of those deep, ingrained evolutionary triggers."

JJ was right, this *is tew* much. What the fuck? My head was spinning. This was all way too much information to process at once. Not to mention, this beautiful ass woman standing next to me made it wet, er- *hard* to think and absorb information.

Gina suddenly goes still like a statue, shoots up in the air, and out of sight. A few seconds later, she returns.

"Cops are coming. You two get out of here. I'll deal with them."

JJ furrows his brow inquisitively.

"Vampire, remember? I can compel the police to go away, then we will get our people in here and get rid of all supernatural evidence. He probably had some pigs on the take anyway, that's why there haven't been any in sight this whole time."

"What about all the humans? Their families need to know they won't be home. Ever."

Shit, here I go with my sensitive ass. I'm about to start fucking crying right in front of the baddest bitch I've ever laid eyes on.

JJ is getting antsy, I can tell because he keeps cracking his knuckles.

"Once our people clean up, we can figure something out. We can't let the humans find out about us. Not yet anyway. The world isn't ready for twerking vampires and stripper werewolves."

She looks me up and down. "Or any other kind of immortals. If you ever find yourself in an unexplainable situation, or some spooky shit pops off, take my number."

Scrambling to pull my phone out of my tits, a piece of spider goo flies through the air and lands on her cheek.

"Oh fuck! My bad."

"They make these things called purses, Asher." JJ pipes up, shaking his head as Gina wipes it off.

"We're gonna go get you one and give the *girls* a break, mmk?"

"Our trailer park is called Dutchville. You should come by sometime. We have the best parties. I promise no one will bite you. Unless you want them to." She flashed a smile, fangs and all.

Damn, she fine. Bite me, baby.

JJ makes a face like he's bitten into a particularly sour lemon.

"And that's my cue to go. Pleasure meeting y'all. Go on and exchange numbers, bump pocketbooks, talk about catfish, and whatever tarnations are. I'll be in the car."

I shove my phone back in my tits, happy as hell I got her number. I'm definitely not letting it go to waste.

"Don't mind him. He's too bougie to function."

Gina laughed adorably.

"Y'all go on ahead. We got this. I'm sure we will be seeing both of you soon."

"ASHER!" JJ yells, pulling me away from my soon-to-be wife. "Po-po coming! Hello! Brown boy over here! If they shoot my ass after all this, I'm haunting you."

Damn his sassy ass, now I'm all confused.

"Umm, yeah, see you soon" is all I can muster.

"Where is your car, bitch?" He yells, shrilly.

"You pussy blocking hoe," I say through clenched teeth. "It's to the right!

"I NEED TO PISS!"

"Your other right!"

I need a dab, like my life depends on it. I start my car and the engine whirs to life. The radio blares, still stuck on my favorite *oldies* station. The chorus to Brandy and Monica's *The Boy is Mine* rattles our ear drums. JJ and I both stare ahead wide-eyed, before we dive to turn the radio off.

"Too soon!" we both yell, exasperatedly.

I put my car in drive, rolling forward when I glance at the rearview mirror and notice some kind of finger bone or metatarsal in my hair.

JJ says, "leather daddy crossing."

I'm so confused right now.

"Asher."

His tone is getting more tense.

"ASHER."

He's screaming now.

"Don't hit that zaddy!"

I slam on the brakes, and a cute ass curly-haired guy in a leather jacket with pants to match walks past. He startles, stopping in front of us before he realizes we weren't going to run him over. He flashes us *both* a winning, *very* toothy grin. We both smile back as he continues to cross, then his arm falls off right in front of us. He bends down to pick it up and uses it to wave goodbye to us.

We both look at each other, saying "Zombie" in unison. Then we pause and blink slowly for a beat.

"You can have him," we both say at the same time again, before we burst out laughing.

"Let's make a pact," I say before we pull off. "Friends forever?"

"For life!" JJ yells.

A shiver runs down our spines, then it disappears as quickly as it came.

JJ checks himself in the visor as we pull around the block.

"This was, hands down, the most fucked up night I've ever had. We must never speak of it ever again." He said, before closing it.

"I don't want to remember. I don't want to know what was real and what wasn't."

We passed the alley behind the building, JJ kept his eyes trained on the darkness within it. A single dot of sweat dripped down his forehead.

"No one would believe us anyway. Exploding discoballs. Immortal douchebags. Monsters in a club."

I shook my head, watching the clurb get further and further away in the rear view mirror.

"In the clurb we're all monsters," I say ominously, deep in thought as the stoplight in front of us filled the car's interior with red light.

JJ gives me the *you are so fucking high* face that his ass always does while he rolls his window down. Before the light turns green, I see a dark figure step out of the shadows and stumble near my car.

"TITLE DROP!" An unhoused gentleman sings, clinging to the passenger side of JJ's best friend's ride.

The vagrant brought his hand close enough to JJ to make him flinch before he dropped a shining golden feather in the car window. JJ's face went pale as he let out a scream so loud and gay that it went from a balloon squeak to a deafening peak, followed by him shrieking,

"DRIVE DRIVE DRIVE!"

The last thing I saw as we gunned it away from our last scare was the unhoused man winking at me. At least, I think that was a wink.

Epilogue Hoe!

Asher

JJ really did spend the entire next day in his bathtub. He facetimed me. What I thought would be pink ended up being brown. Who knew? When his social battery refilled and his fingertips unwrinkled, he left his bat cave to come see me.

Now we're sitting on my couch. I'm in my unicorn onesie. JJ's rocking his gloomy bear onesie, with the ass flap and all. I told him to please, for everyone's sake, wear underwear.

"Let's watch a movie," I say.

"Oh! I have this giallo I want to show you, it's called *Death Wore White After Labor Day*."

"I don't feel like reading subtitles, boo. They make my eyes hurt."

"I haven't seen *But I'm A Cheerleader* in a hot minute," he replies, after some thought.

"Bitch you have made me watch that movie a million times." I roll my eyes at him. "How about Death Becomes Her?"

"Deal. A classic. I'll fight anyone who doesn't love that movie." He says as he gets up to pee.

"Can you throw a bag of popcorn in the microwave after you *wash your hands*?"

"Bitch, this is your Anglo-Saxon house! I ain't the maid." He yells from the bathroom. "And I bet my dick is cleaner than most things!"

I shake my head, trying to remember which of the 40 streaming apps I had that have our movie on it.

"You want me to play the movie or not, hoe?"

"You lucky I was going to get a cookie anyway." He yells over the bathroom sink while running.

"Ayyy, bring those too," I yell back.

He scrunches his facial features, making the *I'm diffi-cult* face, and shakes his ass as he walks into my kitchen.

"Where do you keep your fine china?"

I'm flipping through the channels one last time. I chuckle at his stupid ass.

"Dishwasher," I say, half paying attention to his gay gasping and tutting at me before I stop on a news station.

"Fuck me with a rake, Ma! Why do you leave your knives sticking up in the damn utensil rack? Were you raised by wolves? I cut my damn hand wide the fuck open."

"JAY-JAY!"

"Stop yelling at me. There's blood all over. This is my dick hand, too, dammit!"

He walks out of the kitchen holding his bleeding hand. Looking a little pekid, but still gorgeously tanned.

"Grab some paper towels, don't use my Beetlejuice ones. I will-"

I turn the volume up as the reporter on screen stands in front of Club Hedonia.

"This is ABC Channel 69 with breaking news. A new nightclub, not even past its grand opening weekend, is now the site of a disco bloodbath."

I swear I saw a glint come from JJ's pearly white smile.

They cut to some sergeant.

"We have estimated over fifty casualties. Causes of death are unknown, but we can confirm that the bodies were all dismembered, making it very difficult to identify most of the remains."

The seasoned pig looked like he was going to be sick.

"This morning, we got a report that the roof was ablaze; now all that's left are ashes."

"Oh shit"

The shot cuts back to the news lady on the scene.

"Police are still investigating, but they have removed the deceased and agreed to let us film inside."

She steps back, securing her earpiece, and the camera pans up. Behind her, I see scorch marks where all of our polaroids from that night were displayed. There's only one picture left, undamaged by the fire. My eyes lock on the square with our faces, held in place by a pushpin.

"Ugh, that bitch didn't know her angles at all." JJ scoffs.

"JAY-JAY, you're getting blood fucking everywhere!" I yell, jumping up to help his dumb-boy-brained self.

I freak out when I see his hand filleted, lying open like…well…*I'll just say it. Like a blood-gushing pussy.*

In my shock, I snag my pinky toe on the corner and trip over my gotdamned slippers, tumbling to the floor. I try to catch myself before I hit the floor, but this *ass too juicy.* All my weight landing on my little wrist snapped it, shooting it right through my skin.

JJ shrieks at the sound of cracking celery and tearing flesh.

"MOTHER FUCKERRRRR!" I yell.

It hurts like a sum-bitch. I push myself onto my knees and look at my dangling little appendage.

"Girl, who's going to drive us to the-" he stopped mid-sentence, staring at his hand before he showed me his palm.

The big lipped…*you know what*…is now a little paper-cut, reknitting itself shut before my watering eyes.

He stares at my wrist, and I notice the pain has already faded away. Before I could even turn my hand, we watched in awe as my fractured bones mended and reset themselves, good as new.

"Your hand!" I yell.

"Your wrist!" JJ yells.

"Biiiiiitch!"

We both cackle, before we start twerking in place on my blood-stained hardwood floors.

"Let's hit the clurb!"

<u>THE END.</u>

Phrique's Afterwuuuurd

Wow. So we certainly *did that.* A friendship that grew out of who-the-hell-knows where. I'm not one to question a good thing, though. Alright, that's a blatant lie. Y'all just read a snippet of where my brain is and how far it can go. I'm delightfully unhinged, but it really is cute when I do it.

So when I first had this idea, I thought how fun it would be to take two real-life, actual friends, who are already characters in their own right, and put them on a little adventure. I was a fan of the horror-meets trashy humor that Asher excels at and brought in "Vampire THOTS and Werewolf WAP." I said *it would be funny if...*(p.s., this is how half of my books/stories come about)...hmm, what could I add to this? I mean, besides an abundance of snark, reckless foolery, alliteration, and fancy words? Yet, somehow make it its own entity? Its own fourth-wall-break verse? Why not go for the ultimate fourth wall break? With our real personalities (slightly exaggerated, I would never use the C word IRL), our own vulnerabilities, our own flaws (they have to be some-where, right?), and our own real fears.

Yes, children. I am really not a fan of clowns, nor spiders, which humans have developed an intrinsic aversion to as a survival mechanism after millions of years. Same as clowns, who trigger all the uncanny valley, masked intentions, and unpredictability anxiety we need to say *nope nope nope.* I am also am in fact a psychology under-grad, and a big nerd for evolutionary psychology. I, too, actually develop a fear that I coined *hobophobia.* It was my first ever splatterpunk story, and I will be releasing it soon. Not just because ol' Jerry told me to. Like this story, it means a lot to me because writing my fears out, even humorously, is very cathartic. Also, I'm a dumb Pisces, and my brain really just kinda drags me along for the ride.

This is already too long. Poor Asher is reading this like *JAYJAY whet the hail duz detractor mean??* This was such a fun story to write and read back! I am so glad that I met and became such good friends with my odd couple other-half. She's a tough ol' broad, but she's one of a kind, and I wouldn't want to share my sloppy seconds with anyone else.

Ass-breath.

Asher's AfterTHOTS

Trashy Supernaturals began as just one short story about twerking vampires and then became a whole universe.

I was extremely excited when JJ told me about a collaboration idea with us as the main characters. A trashy Supernaturals side quest? Count me in, hoe!

I never had many friends in my life. I've always been the friend who was easy to cast away and forget about, the sometimes friend. With JJ, it was different. He taught me how positive friendship works. I fell into toxicity, albeit some of my own making, and he grabbed my little sausage fingers and pulled me to the surface. He saved me in more ways than one. He even saved me from myself.

We are extremely different, but we just work. The bougie, hair-flipping word hoe Pisces and the loud-mouthed Mrs. Farts-a-Lot Gemini who can't control her emotions. Even our music tastes are different. Somehow, we just work.

I've had a fear of birds my entire life. I don't know why they freak me out. Maybe it's the death stare or the stabby beak, but I can't stand the feather flappers.

Zombie Nana is a real thing that lives on in my night-mares. When I was five, I started having the nightmare. Now that she has passed away, that nightmare haunts me even more. Sometimes you lose people, and the hole inside of you never gets filled. It's just empty and hollow where their love once resided.

What can I say about spiders? I fucking hate them. BURN IT ALL DOWN. That's my feelings on those eight-legged freaks.

Writing this book was the most fun I've ever had. It sparked something in me that others tried to snuff out.

Breaking the fourth wall was a blast, and yes, I really poop that many times in a day. As I am writing this, I am taking a shit right now.

My sex scene, well, I already know my mama is going to read this, so next family event I will be avoiding eye contact with her at all costs. It's also weird to read about my friend's apparently large gingerbread. Keep it in yo pants hoe.

This has been an amazing few months working on this project with my bestie. Sometimes I get a little heartbro-ken that he is so far away. I don't think Patrick or Dee could deal with us together all the time. Then again I picture them letting us get drunk in our onesies while they yell at us to eat and hydrate.

I've always been a loner, but wanted friends. When you have a bestie that basically equals a whole friend group, you don't really need anyone else. I know you are reading this HOE (JJ). I love you and I appreciate you every day. There aren't really words to express exactly how much you mean to me, and let's be real, you are the one who's great with words. What I'm trying to say is, I'm grateful for our friendship, and I will stab a bitch for you.

Phrique writes phoolery, not at all plain & far from simple. For legal reasons, he only writes what the voices tell him to. He willfully abuses alliteration & injects innuendo where it ought not be, with the intent to make the reader giggle, gasp, and gag at his gaiety. He wants you to laugh at things you shouldn't, so he's not the only one being stared at.

Asher is like if Beetlejuice & Lydia Deetz had a baby & raised it in a creepy quaint trailer park. The little gothbilly puts her heart & her trademark scents in everything she touches. Her ghouls are glamorous, her villains are violent, and her monsters are fearfully fuckable. Once you enter the AsherVerse, you are guaranteed to want to come back now, y'here?

Also by